THE WEREWOLF TRACE

THE WEREWOLF TRACE

John Gardner

Doubleday & Company, Inc.
Garden City, New York
1977

ISBN: 0-385-00543-1
Library of Congress Catalog Card Number: 76-23761
Copyright © 1977 by John Gardner

For
Anton Felton
and
Michael Rubinstein
Friends and Advisors

CONTENTS

Contents

It was known that an organisation for guerilla warfare, the so-called Undertaking Werewolf, had been secretly set under the authority of the now unbiquitous Himmler . . . the Werewolves themselves never expected to have to fight in civilian clothes; they assumed they would fight in uniform, and thus, when captured, be entitled to the treatment of prisoners of war; the discovery that this was not so was responsible for many desertions. Why then were the Werewolves ever regarded as a serious menace?

H. R. Trevor-Roper: *The Last Days of Hitler*

THE WEREWOLF TRACE

Book One:

SPECTRES FROM THE PAST

I

It was only after the British Airways Trident unstuck
from the cold stressed-concrete of Tempelhof that
Cooling wondered if it could be a domestic problem.
The instructions had come through the military, which
was not the usual way for the department to issue orders.

As Berlin dropped into the mists below, and they
headed up the invisible corridor, he wondered if something had happened to his mother. Then reason took
over. If it had been like that they would have given it
to him straight. Hardwicke would have told him to his
face. After all, he was not clandestine. Evaluators—
wall-watchers—were almost classed as civilians. They
had cover, yes, but everyone knew about wall-

watchers. It was strange, though, that such precise orders had come through the military. Report back to London: ticket: flight number. "You'll be met," the young half-colonel had told him, stroking his smooth ginger moustache and not looking terribly happy. All a bit cloak and dagger for an evaluator. It had put the wind up the half-colonel. Probably wondered what he had been harbouring. Vincent Cooling did not like it either.

At Heathrow they picked him up straight away, though he had never set eyes on them before. Pleasant big men, heavies, he supposed, who called each other Bud and Greg, like some old music hall double act.

Bud drove, very smoothly and fast, with that strange brand of intuition which seeks out gaps in traffic long before they become visible.

They came off the M4 and over the flyover just as the light was fading. Cooling saw that the windows of one of the big squat ugly office blocks had been decorated with pieces of cotton wool to simulate Christmas snow. You could see cards on the desks and girls putting on their coats. The thought of Christmas depressed him and the feeling became worse as they hit the Cromwell Road.

He had not been back for six months, and even in that short time things had got worse. More buildings were coming down, fewer going up. For Sale notices sprouted like sad flags along the route, indicators of inflation, and there were blank spaces among the shop fronts, as though some kind of dental decay had set in among the small traders.

As they reached Knightsbridge a police car threaded past, klaxon going, and he caught sight of the tense faces of its occupants. No laughing policemen these days.

"Another bomb," Bud stated. A fact of death.

"Area car," said Greg looking bored. "Mugging, blagging, bomb. Who cares any more?" He shifted round to look at Cooling, whom they had put in the back. "Do they still care in Berlin? Still frolic on the Ku-dam?"

"They still frolic and agitate. But it's quieter than it was. Detente time, isn't it? Enemies making up. Hands across the wall. Where're we going?"

"Didn't they tell you?"

"Just that I had to come back. I haven't anywhere to lay my weary head."

On the last occasion he stayed in London they had put him into one of their larger houses. Three months with an assorted bunch all doing different courses. That was a couple of years ago and, at thirty-one, he remembered feeling an old man compared to the others, fresh-faced and hardly out of their cradles. Three months to do a booster course on the latest surveillance gear. They could have covered it all in a couple of weeks. At the time he had thought it a waste of the taxpayers' money. Three months of electronics, sneakies and cameras which he would never have to use. He had said as much to Gibbs, who told him an evaluator should know exactly how the hardware was handled. In turn he had asked if all doctors had to do a course on armaments and bomb-making. Gibbs stuffily replied, without a smile, that some of their doctors did.

"You're a registered package," grinned Greg. "Very valuable. I expect they've got a luxury penthouse for you."

"James Bond Rules. Okay?" chuckled Bud, sashaying the car neatly between a pair of taxis and negotiating the back-doubles into St. James's. You could hear the wrath of other drivers stranded in their wake.

He realised where they were heading now: in through the maze of streets off St. James's. He had been to the house once before. A year or so ago they had flown him in for the inside of a day. A special operations briefing. Hints of what he should look for: mostly economic and commercial stuff. Another waste of time. Nothing had shown up. He remembered it as a comfortable house with an air of luxury about it, unusual in department premises. He recalled a bathroom done in black tiles and mirrors, and a large dining room with Georgian silver.

They took him straight in (Bud had a key). The recent defence cuts did not seem to have made any appreciable difference to the place. He half expected to see a butler emerge through the door leading from the hall to the nether regions, but it was Gibbs who came out from what he remembered was the study.

"Good." Gibbs stretched out a limp hand, his face creased into a smile which only worked his lips. Their hands met and all the softness went out of Gibbs' hand, his fingers closing like a vice.

"All right?" Gibbs' eyes shifting to the pick-up men.

"Just waiting," Greg nodded towards a trimphone looking incongruous, perched on a console table: a marble top resting on the wings of an eagle. Above it a large gilt-framed mirror.

They're playing Boy Scout games, thought Cooling. Another car at Heathrow following them in. Watching. Their routines were all laced with suspicion.

The trimphone whistled and Greg picked it up, nodding at the voice in his ear.

"Okay," he said, replacing the instrument. Then to Gibbs, "All done. All clear."

They both grinned at Cooling, murmured their good nights to Gibbs and let themselves out.

"Well, Vincent." Gibbs ran his fingers through lank and thinning hair, baring his teeth in the same old smile. Cooling remembered that some people in the section called him "Dentifrice." The teeth were large and patently false, so the nickname was double-edged. "Nice to see you again," he continued. "Hope we didn't play havoc with your social life, shunting you out like this."

"Nothing that can't be mended."

They'd know bloody well that his social life was limited since Steph came back to London. They always knew things like that. It suddenly struck him that he might possibly see her if they kept him in town for more than the odd day. Their parting had hardly been one of sweet sorrow, more of necessity, for Steph had to obey her masters (a multinational company) with the same loyalty, though not the same stealth, as Cooling.

"You won't be going back for a while, I'm afraid." There was a hint of concern in Gibbs' eyes, as though he feared hidden commitments in Cooling's Berlin life.

"I didn't realise. I haven't brought much," Cooling half-gestured, rather hopelessly, towards his hold-all. "I wasn't told it was a posting."

Vaguely he wondered if they were going to be stupid and ship him off to Hong Kong and a China-watchers' course. It was the kind of thing the army did, reclassifying a cook as a driver.

"Your things'll be sent on. Hardwicke's packing up for you."

Cooling felt a small flurry of panic. Was there anything in his room that he would not like Hardwicke to see? Certainly nothing political. Steph's few letters? No, anyone could have read those without interest. Neither of them found joy in written erotica. The thought slid through his head that by now they had probably been read anyway.

"Right, then, I'll show you to your room."

Gibbs was like the owner of a guest house, his attitude stuck midway between the proprietorial and subservient. It was his way of managing things. Cooling knew, from the personal experience of seeing him in action, that Gibbs trod a very careful line, especially where the evaluators were concerned. He had to be delicate, stuck between the department and the military; particularly as the military were almost paranoid about wall-watchers, jealous in the belief that their own intelligence people could do the job more efficiently and with far fewer problems.

He followed Gibbs up the narrow staircase, his eyes taking in the somewhat ragged hem of the checked trousers, and the scuff marks on the old soft shoes, which made no noise on the deep carpet. Gibbs dressed like an absent-minded don, and there were those who maintained that he did so with great care in an attempt to cling to a private legend.

Somewhere in the cellarage there was a noise, as though someone had dropped several metal pans. The crash was followed by raised voices, muffled but angry.

Gibbs made a tutting noise and they turned right, off the landing into a short corridor: three doors to the left, two to the right.

"Bathroom," said Gibbs, touching the first to the right, as though he was playing some children's game in which contact with the door preserved you from a forfeit. They stopped at the middle door on the left.

The room was a mixture of chintz and leather, as

though it housed men and women by turns: an interior decorator's compromise. The two windows were screened by heavy red curtains patterned with huge flowers and hung by the old method, on rings around brass rods.

There was a washbasin, dressing table and wardrobe (in white, matching the wallpaper), a single bed with a small glass-topped table, and an easy chair. It was like a room in a two-star hotel but there was no telephone, radio or Bible. A paperback copy of *England Made Me* lay on the bedside table.

Gibbs hovered in the doorway, muttering something about towels and soap, checking that they were there by the washbasin as though this was his special responsibility.

"Dinner will be in half an hour," he said, glancing at his watch. "I'm that way," pointing up the corridor. "The Deputy Director is staying the night. He'll be in the other one."

So Willis Maitland-Wood was going to spend the night with them. Dine with them also, Cooling fancied. He automatically checked his watch as Gibbs closed the door and padded silently away. No wonder they had been subjected to the Boy Scout games. He noticed the metal framework screwed to the door, half-disguised by the paintwork, and the two recesses, top and bottom, for the security screw locks. He reckoned there would be similar ones on the outside. You could lock yourself in or be locked in.

There was a mirror above the washbasin. Was it a two-way? Doubtful. His face looked back blankly, as though the image did not recognise the reality. It was like a piece of badly carved grey stone, the nose out of true, broken, hair thinning and a little fat gathering along the jowls and under the chin. In a year or two, he thought, this man will be indistinguishable from the mass of desk-toilers on commuter trains, in and out on the production line: middle way, class and brow.

Out of a committed sense of tidiness he adjusted his tie, lightly brushing the lapels of his grey suit: it had always been grey, at school, the university and now, for he dressed out of social habit, having neither the flair nor figure to cut a dash with the elegant fashions of male boutiques. The tie, even was old school, slanting bars of yellow on black, locking him firmly into life's happiest days.

Not a vain man, Cooling was often shocked by the gulf between his reflected outward appearance and the knowledge of the real man: both the truths, habits and elaborate night-time fantasies.

He crossed to the window nearer the bed and pulled back the heavy curtains. There was a net curtain close to the window, hung from a solid rod, its hem weighted and tucked into a shallow trough at the base of the frame. Anti-blast, to stop the flying, spinning fragments of glass. He gently pulled back the netting and peeped out. In the street below cars were parked on either side, leaving only room for traffic to scrape past one

way. At least two of the cars down there would be occupied by surveillance teams. The window frame, like
the door, was re-enforced with a metal screen. Pulling
the heavy curtains again, Cooling turned back into the
room and wondered where the microphones were
hidden.

2

Fine Victorian country residence in charming Surrey village. Five reception; six bed; two bath; kitchen laundry/utility; detached studio; two garages; outbuildings and greenhouse; oil central heating; four acres well-kept garden; immediate possession; freehold; four miles Farnham; one hour plus Waterloo: £48,000 o.n.o.

In fact it took them one hour and five minutes from Waterloo to Farnham, then fifteen minutes in the estate agent's car to reach the village of Tilt and the house with the folksy name of Pine Copse End.

For once they had not driven from London, and for once Joseph had not been fully organized by his secretary, the enigmatic Miss Anerson. At least that was

how Sybil thought of her, though she would be the first
to admit that enigmatic might be the wrong word.

Sybil only saw Miss Anerson on occasional visits to
the office—Scandinavian Imports (Furnishings) Ltd.—
or when the girl brought papers to the flat for Joseph to
sign, though few would argue that Miss Anerson had
that blond and icy beauty which goads men towards at
least considering a defrosting operation.

Reena Hartley, Sybil's neighbor in the service flats
off Kensington High Street, had seen Miss Anerson
once, when Joseph was away from his office with 'flu
during the previous winter.

"Joe's secretary?" she shrieked, raising her heavily
ringed hands in horror (she was an ex-actress with a
string of credits from TV soap operas). "Darling, you
must be out of your mind. You let him work in his own
business next to *that* all day? Watch him like a hawk,
darling, like a swooping hawk."

Sybil rarely gave the matter a thought. There was
too much unsaid and understood between her and Joseph. Besides, as she well knew from their somewhat
unconventional courtship, he was a slow burner in the
matter of physical relationships. She also considered
that there was safety in numbers: there were two other
equally attractive and glacial girls at Scandinavian Imports—Miss Bjornson and Miss Thark. Though from
time to time she wondered at the working of her husband's mind: how he came to surround himself with
long-legged blond beauties in his business, yet in mar-

riage had given himself to her—mouse-haired and of only average height.

She was surprised, on the morning they went down to Pine Copse End, that Miss Anerson had not seen to the details. Joseph even had to go off and buy the tickets at the station. Later, she remembered standing in the main concourse hoping that he was carrying enough money. Usually when he went on a journey, Miss Anerson arranged everything: bookings, tickets, credit cards, cars to meet him, down to the cash in his wallet. For this trip she had done none of these things.

Sybil stood waiting by the do-it-yourself photograph booth, thinking that the display pictures all looked as though they were murder victims, and wondering, for the millionth time, what had prompted Joseph to search out of London for a home. His suggestion, longed for by her, had been unexpected, but so had his proposal of marriage four years before in that ridiculous hotel in Buenos Aires. She realised only later that Joseph had made up his mind to marry her within a few days of their first meeting—at thirty-five thousand feet over the Andes in a Pan-Am jumbo with her serving him free first-class California champagne.

She knew by now that any decision really meant that Joseph had applied himself to the problem, making the decision not really sudden at all. With regard to the house in the country she detected no pondering on his part. It was what she wanted, of course, but she had not, to her knowledge, pushed, probed, hinted or

suggested. His business had to come first and she could
wait a few years, even though she daily grew more disenchanted with the city.

When they came back to Europe, after the honeymoon, and started the business in London, Sybil accepted the fact that they were destined to be city-
dwellers for some time. Maybe, she argued, she would
come to like it. When Helen arrived, two years later,
she hoped that perhaps he would think of moving out
and finding another way. Possibly, she thought, the
subject could be broached as the child grew nearer to
school age.

Then, one evening in July, a week after they returned from nearly a month in a rented villa on Corfu,
he brought it out almost casually as though he was
talking about booking theatre tickets.

"There's something I want to talk to you about,
Angel," he began.

As it happened she actually did think it was to do
with theatre tickets. "Right," she said, and put down
his coffee next to the chair where he had coiled, tense
like a spring, his legs curled under him.

Helen was fast asleep, there was nothing decent on
the television, and it was the maid's night off. She took
her coffee to the leather couch, sat down and waited.

"I have been thinking that perhaps the city is not the
ideal place to live any more." He said it carefully, as
though testing ice on a frozen pond.

She could have gasped with pleasure, but only managed to burble something like, "But you love the city, you always . . ."

"Forget what I always, Angel," the smile so warm she could almost feel it glow on her own face, like a sunray lamp. Before he proposed to her there had never been a single endearment. Once she had accepted, it was Angel all the time. "I am thinking about the future. About you and Helen."

"The bombs?"

He made an irritated noise, as though terrorists played little part in his thoughts. "If it was not the IRA it would be someone else. Urban guerrilla warfare's in vogue. No, it's the quality of life. Don't you feel it also? I don't know how you stick it. The fabric."

She gave a small laugh. "I loathe it."

"Then why don't you tell me? We share most things."

"We don't share the business, Joseph. It's important for us all."

"The business. People commute; they travel to and fro; each day." He shrugged and began to uncoil, the light from the standard lamp falling across his face, glinting on the short fair hair. He looked nearer thirty years old than his forty. "I would not even have to travel every day. If we had the right kind of place, I could have some meetings there, in the country. We could entertain buyers. Miss Anerson can look after much of the office work."

For a moment she wondered if this was a *fait ac-*

compli; that he had already decided on a country re-
treat; even bought the house. "Whereabouts?" She almost expected him to produce the deeds and flourish
photographs.

But he only shrugged and smiled, happy to see that
she was satisfied, relieved that she was also anxious to
get out of the city.

"Anywhere within reasonable distance. I am tired of
the mess of London, Angel. Oh yes, nice restaurants,
good movies, concerts, theatre, but . . ." he swallowed,
shaking his head, "but it's a mess, it'll soon be like New
York, the crush and the filth, the look on people's faces.
It's a powder keg. I say to myself, is this what life is
about? I wish for my little daughter—excuse me, *our*
little daughter—to grow up out of the mess."

Apart from occasional oddities of syntax, Joseph
could be taken for a Briton born. The fair complexion
and short, muscular body could have made him
Scottish. On first meeting him, Sybil had been surprised to discover that he was a Dane.

"You are happy to make the move?"

She nodded and went over to kiss him. "You won't
know how happy."

"It can be a good house. A big house. Big garden. I
shall leave all the décor to you."

"Décor," she repeated, laughing. It was the start of
the search.

They went off every week-end, and on occasional
weekdays, leaving little Helen with the Portuguese

maid, making forays into Kent and Essex, Surrey and Hampshire, looking for a home which did not seem to exist.

Through August and September they traipsed through empty mansions in varying states of repair; they saw well-kept houses, wood rot, rising damp, big rooms, small, and strange-shaped places. But they saw not one from which they could return to London filled with enthusiasm, knowing that they had found home. Not until they took the train to Farnham and the car up to the village of Tilt, and fell in love with the great ugly multigabled, mellow red-bricked Pine Copse End with its huge white barge boards and leaded windows.

There was much that needed doing: some damp problems, complete redecoration, a whole new floor in the drawing room downstairs. But it did not matter. The place drew them to it with an almost mystical call. As well it might, reflected Sybil: she had come a long way from the council house where she had been born, and her father's constant insistence that only the unions would make Britain great again. As she walked through the big hall of Pine Copse End, up the pitch pine staircase, and looked out on the walled garden from the oriel window, in the second bedroom, she wondered what her father would have thought of her. All property, he repeated in life, was theft.

The place had been on the market for nearly two years. Joseph offered £39,000. They held out for a week before accepting.

Helen was left more and more with the maid while Sybil chose papers, material, carpets and took colour schemes to Joseph for approval. Joseph handled the lawyers and the mysteries of conveyancing. It all went very smoothly, and, by the end of November, they knew that they would at least be moved and in—if not quite settled—by Christmas.

3

Willis Maitland-Wood dressed like an old-style Civil Servant: the grey tie, black jacket and striped trousers; the establishment uniform shared also by Harley Street consultants. In fact he could well have been a surgeon: hands white and sensitive; long fingers, well cared for; his hair, helped from a bottle to that total silver grey, laid back from his forehead like an expensive pelt. Smooth; groomed; well-heeled; professional.

"I should imagine it could go either way," he was saying to Gibbs. "We at least have the ear of the Treasury, if not the leverage we once boasted."

He stopped abruptly as Cooling hesitated in the doorway looking at them, strange opposites: the perennial professional man and the leftish don in checked trousers, soft shoes and an old jacket with leather patches on the elbows.

"Ah, Cooling, how nice to see you again," the Deputy Director rose, extending a hand.

They had met officially only three times, yet the greeting was that of an old and trusted friend. Maitland-Wood had, among his many outward facilities, the politician's knack of making one feel known, wanted and among friends. He was, as many observed, an expert with the rapier.

"Drink, Vincent?" Gibbs, who had been leaning against the black mantelpiece—relieved only by an ormolu clock—moved forward to the table, his hand raised over a tantalus which might well have brought a tidy sum at Sotheby's.

Cooling mumbled yes, sherry, dry, and tried to meet the Deputy Director's effusive greeting with equal skill.

They were in what could only be called the drawing room—across the hall from the dining room and study, high-ceilinged with some exquisite plasterwork, lit by a pair of expensive Victorian student lamps and two very military standards with large brass shades all at odds with the electric fire with its fake coals and imitation flames.

"How's Berlin, then, Vincent?" Maitland-Wood neatly picked up the Christian name from Gibbs.

He's being too nice, his vote-catching manner too unctuous, thought Cooling. It worried him, for he was far from being a senior evaluator on the wall. Horsefield and Nash were both his superiors, not to mention Hardwicke.

"Quiet, sir. You'll have read the reports. A really slow year."

"But for the ebb and low of Russian divisions, eh?" Cheerful and all friends together.

"They come and go. Like the trawlers and the Red Sea fleet."

Maitland-Wood looked at him, as though weighing him up. It was not a mental exercise: more the professional eye of the hangman working out his formula, or the undertaker running an eye over a sickly friend. At last he said, "You did very well on that trade thing last month, what was its designation?" The question flung at Gibbs as though a man in the Deputy Director's position could not be expected to remember the trivia of his trade.

"Ploughman," Gibbs muttered, his lips hardly moving.

"We didn't turn up much." Cooling reflected that his report on Ploughman had run to only two pages of what used to be called foolscap.

"Enough, enough." Maitland-Wood stared at his feet. "I often think evaluators should be brought back from time to time and shown the full dossier of operations like that. Give them the range. Let them see the entire panorama: where their pieces of the jig-saw fit in."

Gibbs shook his head. "Insecure. Need to know's always the safest."

The Deputy Director laughed, a silvery chuckle, like

the small kink at the back of his hair. "You're very conservative, Tony—in the best possible sense, of course," another chuckle at his little gibe. "What do you think, Vincent?"

There was a terrible stillness, as though this was a catch question in an oral examination.

"In the main I agree with Tony. I think it could be dangerous. My job is to read the runes. There's such a thing as knowing too much. It could make an evaluator jump to conclusions." He paused. "Is that why I'm here?"

He was aware of Gibbs throwing him a warning look.

"What? To get an over-all view?" This time Maitland-Wood did not laugh, though his lip curled in gentle mocking amusement. "In good time, Vincent. All in good time. I want you to get a new perspective regarding one small problem. A new perspective for me. But all in good time." Smoothly he altered course, swinging the conversation into another channel: chit-chat about Kissinger's Middle East circus, then of a deep penetration operation against the IRA which had gone off at half cock. He named no department names and it was all out of Cooling's area, but fascinating just the same. The Irish operation had obviously been bloody and insecure: they were worried about things getting into the papers—as they always were. "Sometimes I get the feeling that the bloody *Daily Express* knows more than I do," said the Deputy Director.

In the midst of this, a neat grey man in a white jacket, tight across wrestler's shoulders, appeared silkily in the doorway and announced that dinner was served.

After the manner of evaluators, Cooling found himself wondering at the half-heard remark regarding the former lever they had been able to use against the Treasury: filing it away for future reference together with the little learned about the Irish debacle.

Dinner was another world: candelabra, the Georgian silver and five-star cuisine. Greg had said it—"James Bond Rules. Okay?"

During the meal they talked non-department chaff, clear of politics: an overpraised thriller, the danger of teeny-bopper indiscipline, the horrors of all-embracing comprehensive education (Maitland-Wood had a daughter at some mixed place) and, last, the films of Ken Russell. Cooling had not read the thriller, agreed with regard to the teeny-boppers and comprehensive education but had never seen one of Ken Russell's films. Throughout the bulk of the meal he tried observation evaluation techniques on the slaves—two elderly Middle-Europeans who, he considered, were security cleared as far as Gabriel. He also watched his companions and their methods of eating: Maitland-Wood the hearty trencher-man, elegant but fast; Gibbs precise, cutting everything into similar parcels which were deposited into his mouth as though by a carefully adjusted machine, then chewed at a standard rate.

Just before the port, Cooling realised with a shock that he had met Maitland-Wood on four occasions, not the remembered three. It knocked him off balance for a second, particularly as the realisation came to him without warning. The Deputy Director had been at his Foreign Service interview—on the board.

Memory, he knew only too well, was selective, that was part of his stock in trade, yet he could not understand why the fact had eluded him for so long. The connection was obvious, for the link in his mind was Gibbs.

In his last year at Cambridge, Cooling had made a positive decision to try for the Foreign Service, and when the result of his degree was announced he had applied straight away. The first two hurdles—the examination and the forty-eight-hour series of tests—seemed to bode well. Then came the board at the big house in Burlington Gardens. A week later he had the final result by letter. It was couched in official phraseology, which did not help. They were not of the opinion that he was Foreign Service material. That afternoon, Gibbs turned up, out of the blue, suggesting that the Government would be pleased to give him another kind of job.

Now at eleven years' distance, it was all very clear: a normal way of recruitment. He wondered if, perhaps, he had for all these years been the Deputy Director's blue-eyed boy: a kind of interdepartmental sleeper about to be activated now by Prince Maitland-Charming-Wood's kiss of life.

The thought perturbed him. It had always been clearly understood that he did not wish to serve with the blood and thunder brigade which came under the direct authority of Maitland-Wood and those like him.

The table was cleared and the Middle-Europeans disappeared. The stage seemed set and, still lost a little in the maze of possibilities surrounding Maitland-Wood's presence on the Foreign Service board, Cooling gradually became aware that the Deputy Director was once more launched into politics.

"We in the department have to walk a very hairy knife edge," he was saying. "Our lords and masters govern us with a technical majority, and as though they have the most decisive mandate in political history. The opposition sit tight and wait for the chaos. In the meantime the unions lead us by the nose . . ."

"And are in turn led by Moscow?" suggested Gibbs, an eyebrow lifted, presumably to overscore the idea that he was in a goading mood.

"So the Tory Press would have us believe." Maitland-Wood gave a small, unconvincing snort of laughter. "Put Moscow in London and the union sheep wouldn't know what had hit 'em."

"Come and watch the Germans with me," Cooling tried, vainly anxious to let them know that he was still there. "Watch them on both sides of the wall. They're like regimented beavers. Next to the Germans we appear as the most slothful of countries."

"Ah, the English vice of sloth." Maitland-Wood gave a smile as insincere as a cheap television commercial. "You must remember, Vincent, that sloth has always been the cover of the English ruling classes. The problem these days is that our present masters imagine that it is a necessary adjunct of power. Nobody ever bothered to tell them that the old-style men of clubland were only pretending: that behind the yawns and inactivity of the public image lurked much bustle. To be indolent at the lathe is really a mortal sin. To appear to be indolent is cover. But we're not here to discuss the follies of those who lead on the political front."

"What are we here to discuss, then, sir?" Cooling had always been direct, a legacy from his stolid Yorkshire father.

Maitland-Wood did not flinch. "Something very sensitive." He rose. "Something we should discuss in a more workmanlike atmosphere."

They followed him, as though by some prearranged signal, out of the dining room, turning right into the study.

It was much as Cooling remembered it: the maps and projection screen, armchairs lining the wall, a large table serving as a desk on which rested a battery of telephones. The bookcase, he reckoned, was a fake— far too deep: probably a radio housing. Possibly they used the place to conduct delicate operations: away from the prying eyes of Whitehall. In the new climate, the department was not the most popular of outfits.

Suspicion breeds suspicion; security breeds hyper-security.

The Deputy Director waved them into chairs and leaned his plump, well-tailored buttocks against the edge of the desk.

"I have a file," he announced, like a consultant telling his team that he had a patient with some rare and interesting disease. "Only a few people—a very few people—subscribe to it, and those who put it together are either dead or cannot possibly realise the significance of their contributions."

"Like evaluators?" Cooling asked flatly.

"Exactly like evaluators, each dealing with a small piece and with no way in which to view the whole picture. It is the whole picture in which I am interested. I want you, Vincent, to evaluate the entire thing and prescribe action. If necessary, even mastermind action."

"Why me?" Cooling already felt the shudder creeping from his darkest thoughts.

"You're not afraid of responsibility, are you?"

"It depends, sir." He accented the sir. "I don't like being mixed up with the clandestine side."

"Why you?" repeated Maitland-Wood as though mulling it over.

"It's really rather ultra-sensitive," added Gibbs as though he couldn't bear to be neglected.

"I think you will understand better once you've seen

the material. Read the file." The Deputy Director was not looking at him. Talking to the shine on his shoes.

"There are some obvious reasons. Others are less obvious. Believe me, we do sincerely think you are the man to do it."

"I'm not a cowboy." He knew that he was lost before battle was even joined.

"Nobody is suggesting that you are. You may not be the most senior evaluator we have in Germany, but it is our considered opinion that you would be the most astute in the present circumstances. I want you to read the file tonight. Here. With Tony Gibbs present, though I don't want you to discuss it with him."

"But he's my section controller."

"I am well aware of that." There was no friendliness in the Deputy Director's voice now. Do not presume with me, young Cooling, he seemed to be saying.

"Nevertheless you will not discuss it with Tony Gibbs. Not tonight. Tomorrow we'll go over the whole thing. He's here merely to watch," a frosty smile, "and watch over you. It should take you three, four hours to read, mark and learn. Now, if I were you, I'd go and make yourself comfortable."

"We'll be locked in," said Gibbs as though agog at the idea of a secret so huge that it had to be read behind bolted doors.

"In the meantime I'll call up the file."

Cooling rose and started towards the door. There was no point in arguing.

"What beverage, Vincent?" asked Gibbs.

For a moment he did not understand.

"Tea or coffee? We're going to be in here for some time."

"Oh yes, coffee for me."

As he left he could hear Maitland-Wood dialling. He did not even turn around to see which telephone was being used. Walking upstairs to the black-tiled bathroom with the mirrors, Vincent Cooling felt even more uneasy. It was the Boy Scout games again. Big secrets, the file being escorted into this well-watched gilt and gingerbread house. He had always tried to stay apart from the big secrets because inevitably they became the preserve of the blood and thunder boys. He wanted nothing of that.

Downstairs again a percolator had appeared, bubbling with coffee, and there was a tray with cups and the usual accessories.

"I want you to read it straight and with an open mind," the Deputy Director said. "Try and sort the wheat from the chaff so that you can give me a snap opinion in the morning. Then we can go into more detail."

The uneasiness bloomed inside Cooling. They all took the games so seriously. Deadly.

Somewhere in the house a bell rang and Maitland-Wood was striding towards the door. The file was here: and now.

4

When Sybil Walters reached over to pour the California champagne for Joseph Gotterson—thirty-five thousand feet over the Andes, almost five years ago—marriage was far from her mind.

Having reached her late twenties, she had done what she set out to do in her teens. She was independent, free within the strictures of her job, well paid, had travelled, seen life and enjoyed herself to the full.

"Education," her father used to say, "is the right of every human being, not the prerogative of the rich. You will have education, Syb, use it for the future."

As much as she was later at odds with that fat, overbearing, red-faced man, she had taken his advice, though hardly in a way that he would have wished.

To a bright girl, the eleven plus examination (at that

time the final judgement on a child's future) had been simple and, to a large extent, she had found pleasure in seeing her parents' pride when she started her first term at the Grammar School.

Yet hearing her father's repeated doctrines each evening, and observing the world from within the Girls' Grammar School walls during the day, gradually wore down her tolerance. By the time she reached the fifth form she was not at all certain that the country's future lay in the hands of her father's precious unions; nor was she altogether convinced that a shift to one-party political power was for the good of all men. To be truthful, she discovered that she was not really interested in her father's politics. There was far more that her education could do for her. The glossy advertisements, the possibility of life beyond the class struggle of her parents' kitchen, the lure of the big stores with nice clothes, and fascinating pleasures all around were far stronger than the thought of fighting some dreary battle for the sake of those who were not prepared to work for themselves. All men, she wrote in her O Level History paper, are not equal, and no political power on earth can make them so.

Her teachers dearly wanted her to go on into the sixth form and then to university. Her father pleaded with her (seeing her, perhaps, as a latter-day crusading socialist lady). But she had her own ideas, and at eighteen she was accepted for training as an air hostess in the, then, British Overseas Airways Company. "Why,

Syb, why?" her father asked, furious and frustrated while her mother got on with the household drudgery which had been well marked by Sybil. She was determined not to follow in mother's or father's footsteps. "You'll be a superannuated waitress. A lackey," her father shouted angrily on the first day she started work.

She did not view it in that light at all. For several years she shared a flat in London with three other girls. She did not particularly care for the work—which was, she had to admit, much as her father described it—but the rest of her life amply made up for that. She had begun to move on from the class struggle her father saw so clearly (and from a biased viewpoint). She travelled, learned much, and eventually took herself out of the care of BOAC and into the arms of their largest American competitor, Pan-Am.

For a while she worked out of London. Then, later, from New York. She had been on the long run south, on the Latin American route, for six weeks when she came into collision with the clear, somewhat cold blue eyes of Joseph Gotterson.

She did the trip once a week, with a one-night stopover in Buenos Aires. Crews stayed at a comfortable, though ridiculously elaborate, hotel and it was in the main bar that she bumped into her former passenger.

"You were on the airplane," he said shyly.

"Why yes. Mr. Gotterson?"

She was in fact waiting for the rest of the crew, warm in the knowledge that the captain was making a big play for her. The rather timid man with the blue eyes and fair complexion was really more interesting. Captains were a dime a dozen—a phrase those gentlemen often used about stewardesses.

She accepted a drink from the quiet Mr. Gotterson, then dinner. He was more than ten years her senior, a Dane whose parents had died in the war. He had been brought up by a wealthy uncle here in Argentina, though he passionately wanted to return to Europe and run his own business, the nature of which remained unspecified. No, he did not like South America, but felt that he could not leave altogether until his uncle was dead. Later she discovered that the old man was already near death. He was painfully shy, unassuming yet attractive. When the evening came to an end he shook hands with her rather gravely. This was a new experience. Men with old-fashioned courtesy were unknown to her.

The association developed almost casually. Within a few weeks she would find Joseph regularly waiting for her at the airport, his manner kind and correct. He bought her flowers and occasional small gifts. After a couple of months she went down with some little virus and was unable to fly for a week. That was the start of the telephone calls, long and attentive from his uncle's ranch.

Still he made none of the amorous moves she came to expect from male companions, so that Sybil even began to wonder if there was something wrong with him. Or her.

Then his uncle died.

Two weeks later, during the usual stopover, he appeared more nervous than usual. She probed gently and at last, with great embarrassment, he told her that he was returning to Europe within the month. He would be more than honoured (she teased him about it later) if she would come with him as his wife.

Her reaction was instinctive. So much so that she went through hours of soul-searching afterwards. But three weeks later, Sybil Walters became Sybil Gotterson, seen off by all her old Pan-Am friends on a honeymoon in Rome, Venice, Lisbon and all points in between. After the honeymoon they went to Copenhagen for a month while Joseph made the business arrangements, and then to London, where he opened Scandinavian Imports (Furniture) Ltd., complete with Miss Anerson, Miss Bjornson and Miss Thark.

In the second year of the marriage, Helen was born and, to Sybil's surprise, she discovered that Joseph had become a British citizen (he believed, he told her, that the mother was the closest parent to the child, and as she was English and they were to live in England, the father should to all intents and purposes become English also).

From the council house to a beautiful and expensive London apartment was a lengthy stride. Four years after she had accepted Joseph's proposal, Sybil knew that her instinct had not let her down. She had a husband who provided for her in a manner she could never, in her wildest dreams, have thought possible. He was as attentive as any man could be, and her little girl, though a lively handful, was a source of constant pleasure.

It was like a fairy tale; a woman's magazine story; a TV soap opera. Too good to be true; and now there was this splendid house in the country, a stolid buffer against the social unrest of their time. Occasionally she wondered if it was too good to last. She felt no guilt at being what her Women's Lib friends called "sexist." It was what she wanted.

Though Pine Copse End was far from ready, they made the physical move a week before Christmas. The outside and the porch had been painted. The hall was stripped bare and undecorated, with the wires for the light brackets hanging out of holes and taped up for safety. Naked bulbs hung where the chandeliers would go, bathing the patched walls and bare boards in a clear odd light. The kitchen was finished, as was the huge drawing room with the large bay window which looked out onto the terrace and the long garden sloping away, walled on all sides, to the copse from which the house got its name. Upstairs, the main bedroom, one bathroom and Helen's room were completed. Marina, the Portuguese maid slept in a makeshift room next to the nursery, and, in spite of the feeling of impermanence, they were determined to enjoy Christmas in the country and within the walls of their new home.

Until now the house had been owned by only two people: the man who had built it, and his daughter, who had died at some great age only three years before. The daughter had dabbled in art and was a memorable village character. Her studio, built in the late thirties and connected to the house by a short passage, was reached through a door in the drawing room. Joseph was already making this his own: bookshelves had been installed and he had ordered furniture, chosen carefully from his own company, for he considered that the largest part of his work could be done from the house.

On this particular evening he was pottering around, making notes and measuring the shelves to make certain that his newly bought stereo system would fit into them without further problems. Sybil found him working out angles.

"Can you come and see what I've found in the morning room?"

They had christened it the morning room rather grandly, for it was really a small sitting room to the right of the hall, just below the stairs.

"If I place the speakers here, Angel, I will get a beautiful effect when seated at my desk there." Joseph showed her where he had marked the shelves, as though he had not heard her plea. Then, "What in the morning room?"

"Come and see."

He shrugged, not happy about leaving what was to be his particular domain.

She led him through the drawing room with its rust curtains chosen to pick out the highlights in the carpet, and the new deep velvet suite; the picture lights burning above the Lowry. They crossed the hall, moving from relative luxury into the odd emptiness, then to the small room which was stripped and bare, smelling of fresh paint: the woodwork had been completed that afternoon. Like the hall the walls of the morning room were bare and patched, the unshaded light harsh upon them.

"Down here." She pointed towards a corner, across the room by the small arched window. "I saw it as soon as I came in. It's funny, darling, I didn't remember seeing it before."

They went over, kneeling to examine it more closely. Low on the wall, almost touching the skirting board, was a beautifully executed pencil drawing: an eagle, its wings outstretched and talons grasping an indistinct object like a piece of rag. If you looked closely you could even imagine it as something more. The wingspan reached over a good fourteen inches, the whole finely detailed: ruffled feathers and a glint in the bird's eye. The strangest thing was that the whole drawing had been executed upside down, so that the top of the head lay parallel to the skirting, the talons with their indistinct quarry pointing towards the window.

She glanced up at Joseph, who had gone very still, his eyes perceptibly widening. Then, after a good minute, he spoke.

"Remarkable, Angel. One of the workmen, the decorators, must be an artist. It will be covered by the paper though. The wallpaper."

"Yes." She was uncertain, not really knowing why. "Yes, I expect that's it, but somehow it looks older, as if it's been there a long time."

"I did not notice it before."

She looked at him sharply, for his voice had taken on an unaccustomed edge, a brusqueness unusual for him.

"They should not be allowed to waste their time," he said, and she turned towards him again, noticing that his face had hardened, as though marked by anger. "I will speak with them tomorrow." He was indeed angry. "The walls are not here to be drawn upon."

"Oh, come on, darling. It'll be covered up by the paper, you said so yourself. There's no harm done."

"That's not the point, Angel. It's the waste of time that matters. I pay good money, but not for them to waste the time. That's the trouble with this country, too much shirking." He put his arm around her, as though in a protective gesture, still looking at the eagle.

"It's rather good though, isn't it?" She tried to make

light of the whole thing. "I mean he's got talent. To do it upside down as well."

Joseph nodded, calming at her voice. "Well executed, but I do not like it. There's something about it that is unpleasant. The claws."

"Talons."

"The talons. Unpleasant." He turned away, shepherding her from the room.

She admitted to herself that he was right. There was something unpleasant about it, the thing held by the talons, strange, and trailing. A piece of flesh? Some human part? A baby? The thought disturbed her, and a short time later she went upstairs, creeping into Helen's nursery to peep at the little head with its crown of gold hair, peaceful on the pillow.

How was it that small children could look such angels in repose? Helen had been a fiend all day: getting into everything, inquisitive and interested in all that was going on. Now it seemed she could do no wrong, like a cherub from a religious Christmas card. Sentimental maybe, but very real here in the warm nursery with its scent of baby powder and shampoo.

Sybil left the nursery, reassured by the peace of her sleeping baby, going through to the main bedroom to draw the curtains. As she did so she thought she could hear a sound from outside among the trees growing close to the house. A rustle of great wings among the branches. She told herself it could only be the wind, but at the same moment there seemed to be a small cry, like an animal in pain.

She felt chill, a shudder passing through her body, emanating from the sudden churn of fear in her stomach. Undoing one of the window catches, she softly pushed the casement open a few inches, cocking her head to listen.

Only the gentle soughing of the branches came from the black of the night garden.

Closing the window again, she saw clearly in her mind the drawing of the eagle. This time it was the right way up and she knew what was held in its talons. The fear was real and undisguised. A fear she had known was present almost from the moment of her marriage to Joseph; the fear of happiness found being suddenly and irrevocably lost through some strange quirk of fate. It blossomed gently into a constant anxiety as though there was some inevitable tragedy waiting and brooding around the corner of time.

5

Tony Gibbs lolled in an armchair close to the two-bar electric fire, chain-smoking evil-smelling black cheroots. The aroma was nauseating to Cooling, who did not smoke. Gibbs, he noticed, was reading a novel. The rest was silence.

The file lay on the desk in front of him. Like a time bomb, he thought, wondering if he should examine it carefully from the outside before working through its contents.

It was bulky enough, between one and two inches thick: red, with a small pink seal in the top right-hand corner of the cover. The papers within were all blue: standard, neatly typed copies of destroyed originals. He presumed they had all been pulled from microfilm. That was how they usually handled the highly classified stuff. In the margins there were occasional comments in ink.

The first page was of heavier, white paper, giving the file's number and a whole series of cross-references, from which he deduced the contents had been extracted from a wider batch of files.

As Maitland-Wood had suggested, the subscription list was very small. The Director: the Minister; Deputy Director and Gibbs (who had been added barely a week ago). There was a space left for Cooling's own initials, to be appended once the material was read. Beneath the subscription list was a final cross-reference. *Cryptonym Key in Black Book D: Director Only.* It was going to be a crossword puzzle full of unbeatable coding and trick names: a *roman à clef*.

The next page gave the clear designation. Cooling's heart sank. *Trace Reports on Nazi War Criminals.* Dear God, it was thirty years on: had they not yet stopped playing this game? The few left were old old men or, at best, settled into middle age. In any case, the British had never been obsessive about tracking down their enemies, hounding them to prison or the hangman. Some, like Simon Wiesenthal—the most tenacious Nazi-hunter of them all—said it was to their shame that the British did not seem concerned that the murderers of millions should be free and unpunished. Cooling felt little either way. What good could it do now? He understood the Jewish motivation but believed that, unless there was something which really affected the here and now, there was no point in the chase. What could there possibly be after all these years?

He flicked through the pages to familiarise himself with the time span. April 1945 to only a few weeks ago. Merciful heavens, are we so emasculated as a service that our time has to be spent raising ghosts? Probing the past? Eleven years ago, when they had trained him, this kind of material was used for examination and exercise. His formal and final exam had been to run a detailed trace on all those who had been with Hitler in the bunker at the end of April 1945. It had been a good and interesting exercise.

With a sigh, Cooling began the journey.

It appeared to be just as he feared: field trace reports on senior SS men and other "interesting" Nazis. In a way academically absorbing, for here was proof that, in the days immediately following the German defeat, the department had known a great deal more than it ever admitted. When he had done the Führerbunker exercise, for instance, none of this material was available to him.

He reflected that there were many people, particularly former DPs and dedicated Nazi-hunters, who would give their eye teeth for a squint at this little lot. Wiesenthal, and men like him, had a right to moan. In the years before the formation of the State of Israel we had been too busy fighting a pointless colonial rearguard action in Palestine to worry about those who had done their best to destroy an entire nation. It was our small Vietnam; the old guard clinging on in the face of common sense. Just like the rerun we were now seeing in Northern Ireland. Palestine had ended in a kind of defeat, just as Vietnam had been a defeat for America, and Northern Ireland would finally see an exercise in face-saving. All that would be left were men and women mourning the dead. But it was like that with all empires. They rotted from the inside, erupting in boils and pustules which had to be cut away.

The irritating thing about this file was the way in which both hunters and hunted were obscured by the fog of cryptonyms. Trilby reported that Otto was living on a farm in Gaishorn; Ferry spoke of an escape route through Austria to Italy and Spain, already followed by Moonlight and Werewolf; there was another leading from Germany straight to South America: Cutpurse and Falstaff had travelled that one. Orlando reported a conversation concerning Detective. Ahab rendered a report on Scarab. On and on, through the years—out of the forties, into the fifties, through the sixties: tiny pieces of information which meant little unless you could latch on to the real names of Otto, Moonlight, Werewolf, Cutpurse, Falstaff, Detective, Scarab and the like.

Before the early fifties, each of the reports was marked firmly *No Action: File*, with the Director's initials against the rubber stamp; the initials, like everything else, altering suddenly as the chair was vacated and everyone moved up a space. Later, some reports showed a mellowing attitude. *Action: Forward to Shin Beth*—the Israeli Security Service. A new harmony? It also pleased Cooling to see that he was able to pinpoint some of the names. For instance, Doctor, Night Nurse and Consultant were the three most famous of all: names that should be recognisable to any evaluator, in whichever sector he worked. Mengele, Bormann and Eichmann.

The file also revealed how much the department knew, and had known at the time, about Spinne and Kameradenwork, the truly active Nazi underground escape organisations, so often confused with the more free-lance and flashy ODESSA, beloved of fiction writers.

In spite of himself, Cooling found that he was becoming interested, and, once past the half-way mark, he suddenly realised that this file was not simply a haphazard series of trace reports. Slowly, even insidiously, it became plain that they were dealing with two names and two only. Moonlight and Werewolf. The remaining reports were in part padding and in part a crossing of paths.

He went back over the ground again, trying to identify the pair. After all it appeared their journey had started from the very heart of the collapse of the Third Reich: in the Führer-bunker itself, beside the Reich Chancellery, in April 1945. Cooling prided himself that he knew that source as well as anybody. In his head he ticked off names. Those who had died in the bunker.

Those who had escaped and been traced, dead or alive. Those who were still missing. He tried to reassemble the whole cast in his head: Bormann, Zander, Krebs, Freytag von Loringhoven, Boldt, von Below, Weiss, Weidling, Baur, Beetz, Mohnke, Axmann, Naumann, all the way through, mentally reaching back for the entire cast list of that bizarre, Wagnerian and unreal grand finale of the Third Reich.

But he could place neither Moonlight nor Werewolf, and some of the reports appeared to make little sense. In safe exile, for instance, Moonlight appeared to be growing older, even ailing from time to time—as was natural—while Werewolf was reported more and more as leading an active life, the life of a happy young man. No sign of middle age holding him back. It made no sense until, suddenly, Cooling sat up, shocked and full of disbelief. The trace reports had reached the late sixties when out of nowhere came two interrogation snippets quite out of chronology.

The first was dated as early as January 1947. By a senior department officer, frustratingly designated Cobra, it concerned a German who had been brought into the British Field Security Service post in Admont, which also contained one of the largest DP centres in the British Occupied Zone of Austria.

Cobra was there by accident, in the middle of running a terminal trace on several department network agents who had not surfaced since the end of hostilities.

The German had been picked up on the deposition of two Polish DPs who claimed that he had been one of the guards at Dachau. They accused him of nothing but claimed that he was witness to various acts of atrocity. He was, in fact, quickly identified as an *Unterscharführer*—a corporal in the SS. Yes, he had served in the WVHA—that section of the SS responsible for concentration camps—but until the end of 1944 he had been concerned only with administrative work. In Cobra's report he was called Shallow. Someone in the department, Cooling observed, was well into Shakespeare.

As it happened, the FSS released Shallow after a few days, but Cobra was present at his lengthy interrogation and the section of his report now before Cooling concerned Shallow's work during the battle for Berlin. In the last three months of the war, Shallow claimed he was on a special detachment in Berlin under the command of a major, whom Cobra designated Moonlight.

At last there was substance, if not form, to moonlight. Cooling felt a prickle at the back of his neck. He could well guess at the duties of the special detachment. There were grisly stories concerning the flying military courts condemning troops and civilians alike, in the streets of Berlin, and carrying out the sentences on the spot: hanging people quite arbitrarily for treason and cowardice.

His mind fleetingly reflected on Werewolf, also, for that was the operational name given to German parti-

sans of the time: men, women and children carrying
out ambush techniques against the enemy. A connection perhaps?

During the last week in April, Major Moonlight had
ordered Shallow, and another corporal, to come with
him to the Führer-bunker close by the Reich Chancellery. They arrived, he thought, about the nineteenth
or twentieth, and were quartered in the bunker occupied by Brigadeführer Mohnke (Commandant of the
Chancellery) and his staff. On the day of their arrival,
Moonlight spent some time with Hitler and, later, a
considerable time with Goebbels.

Shallow's report continued:

> In the morning the Major told us that we were
> to watch a small ceremony but we were to keep
> out of sight. The Führer was presenting the Iron
> Cross to some of the troops defending the city.
> They were children. Frightened children in uni-
> form. One of them, a nice little boy, had put an
> enemy tank out of action single handed. He was
> in shock. I do not think he knew what was happen-
> ing. The Führer smiled at him, patted his head
> and fondled his face. When he did that, the Major
> said, "Right, lads, that's the one. Don't let him
> leave. But be gentle with him."
>
> The Führer pinned the medals on the boys and
> told them to go back to the defence of the city.
> Then he left and returned to the bunker. The

Major nodded to us and we all went over to the little boy. The other boys were preparing to leave. The child could hardly speak—shock and emotion —he was in a terrible state. The Major said to him, "Here, we're going to give you something to eat. Don't go back with the others. We'll look after you." We took the boy to our bunker. We had a room there, just for myself and the other corporal. We kept the little boy there: gave him food and drink and let him sleep on one of the bunks. One of us stayed with him day and night. All the time he was there he only spoke to say, "Thank you." Poor little devil. We stayed there for a long time.

On the thirtieth, late in the afternoon, the Major came down and told us that the Führer was dead. All hell was breaking out. The shells were coming down near the bunkers, and inside there was a party going on. Everyone had gone crazy. The Major said that the boy was now his responsibility: as for us, it was every man for himself. He took the boy away. I went off to the canteen to join in the fun. We knew it was all over for us. I got drunk with the rest. I think I stayed drunk for about twenty-four hours.

That evening—it would be the next day—those of us who were left talked about making a run for it and I went over to the Führer-bunker to see what was going on. I was half-way there when the shelling started up again, worse than ever, so

*I turned back. As I was turning I saw the Major
hurrying out of the Reich Chancellery garden. He
had the boy with him. I called out but they did
not hear. I did not see them again. It struck me as
being very strange. I left the bunker about an hour
afterwards.*

Very strange, thought Cooling. Another piece of the
jig-saw. No wonder he had not been able to identify
Moonlight. If there was any truth in it, Moonlight was
an SS *Sturmbannführer* on special detachment in Berlin at the end of the war, and on the run, between
bunker and bunker, during the last few days. It was
doubtful, then, if his name appeared in any records:
except, of course, in the Director's *Black Book D.*

What, then, of Werewolf? One of the Hitler Youth
decorated by Hitler towards the end? They had all
seen that film: Hitler looking aged, his eyes haunted as
he smiled at the little row of boys, so proud and yet so
frightened. The caressing hand, the nod of approval.
Still no sense.

Cooling passed on to the next page. This was an even
more tenuous report, dated August 1963. Basically it
concerned a low-grade defection. A Russian non-
commissioned officer had leaped over the wall and
sworn new allegiance to the West. In fact, it was soon
established, he was on the run from disciplinary action:
something to do with a girl and money, the normal

kind of domestic disruption which occurs in armies the world over. As usual in cases like this, the military had been ruthless: a promise to the Russian authorities for a search and return operation. They had him all the time, of course, taking him apart. In short, they dried him out and tossed him back. Though not before letting the department have a go.

A pair of confessors were flown in, and the report in front of Cooling now was a small question-and-answer section of the interrogation. He noticed that it had been evaluated at the time and initialled AG. Tony Gibbs?

With a heavy sense of humour they had coded the Russian Jumper. Cooling thought it was a pity Shakespeare had left the scene.

The section included in the file concerned Jumper's activities during ten months between August 1952 and May 1953, when he was attached for guard duties at Vladimir Prison. Cooling knew all about Vladimir: one hundred and fifty miles from Moscow: old, dreaded and particularly bad. A stopping-off place for those political prisoners who, immediately after the revolution, were forced to march to Siberia. More recently a cold hell-house for other kinds of political miscreants. Greville Wynne, the British courier, had served a large part of his sentence there, though he was one of the lucky ones, for few people ever came back from Vladimir.

They had questioned Jumper most carefully about the prisoners who had been there while he was attached. Here, they were concerned with a German.

Q: Yevgeni, we want to talk about the German you mentioned yesterday. The one you became quite friendly with.

J: Hottzi?

Q: That's him. Do you remember his full name?

J: I think it was Hottzeimer.

Q: You gave the impression you established quite a relationship with him. That was a bit strange at Vladimir, wasn't it?

J: It was, but he was a trusted prisoner. He worked in the Guard House. Mainly dealing with the German documents.

Q: What language did you use?

J: I have German. We spoke in German.

Q: And why was he there? What sentence was he serving?

J: I don't know. Crimes against the State. You can never really tell unless it's a big case—one everybody knows about.

Q: You didn't ask him?

J: We stayed off that. We talked about the past. He talked about his family who had died in Berlin and about his war service. I talked about my service and my family.

Q: Yesterday you said he claimed to have been near Hitler at the end.

J: He said he was in Hitler's bodyguard.

Q: He was SS?

J: I understood so, yes.

Q: He mentioned Begleitkommando.

J: Yes. (*Evaluator's note. An Oberscharführer Ritter Hottzeimer appears on the extant list for the Begleitkommando 1944*).

Q: Good. What did he tell you about those last days?

There followed long, remembered descriptions of the bunker and its occupants. Nothing that was not already known. Until—

Q: Was there anything that struck you as strange about Hottzi?

J: Not strange really. He had a way of suggesting that he knew more than he told us.

Q: In what way?

J: He said there were things that happened on the last days—on the day Hitler died, and the rest —that nobody but a chosen few knew about.

Q: He suggested that he was one of the chosen few?

J: Not really. It was as though he had found something out by accident. In a way he was afraid of it.

Q: Did you believe him?

J: I believed everything else he said. He was very graphic in his descriptions. It all sounded as though he had been there.

Q: No, I mean the thing that he knew and few others did. What about that?

J: I would say that he knew something.

Q: Did you report this to anyone?

J: Yes, to my captain.

Q: And what did he say?

J: He said it was a bit of bravado. Hottzi was trying to make himself into a big man.

Q: Did he question him?

J: The captain? No.

Q: Now, Yevgeni, did he ever give you more than a hint of what his secret was?

(NOTE: The subject took some time before answering. It was a definite altering of pattern in the exchange).

J: Well, yes. He said that on the last day, or sometime in the evening, there was some kind of substitution.

Q: What did you make of that?

J: I think he meant that someone got away from the bunker.

Q: A substitution?

J: Yes, I think he meant a body was left in the bunker dressed as one person, while the real person got away.

Q: Really? Someone important?

J: I think so.

Q: As important as Hitler or Dr. Goebbels?

J: That's stupid. Everyone knows that they were dead. The bodies were identified.

Q: All the bodies of importance were identified. If this so-called substitution was successful they *would* be identified, wouldn't they?

J: I suppose so.

Q: Then why not Hitler or Goebbels?

J: They were dead. He described to me how they died.

Q: Then who could it be? One of the generals?

J: I don't know. This is not important surely?

Q: Did he not say anything that would suggest a name to you?

J: No. He said there was a substitution. Someone was brought in to die in the place of someone else. He said that it was an investment for the future.

Q: He said that?

J: What?

Q: That it was investment for the future? He used those words?

J: Christ, yes. He was always saying it, as if he was repeating something learned by heart. Germany has an investment for the future.

Q: *For* the future, or *in* the future?

J: Both. I don't know—*for* the future, I think. But maybe it was an investment in the future.

Q: But he said it about this so-called substitution?

J: Yes, I think so. Does it really matter?

Q: Did he have any other expressions he used a lot? Like the investment one?

J: When he talked to me about the substitution?

Q: Yes.

J: He didn't really talk about it a lot, you know. It was hinting at it most of the time. An investment for the future. Yes, he did have another saying. There was really room in the world for the substitute. Look, does this matter? Is it important?

Q: Maybe. Maybe not.

In the margin there was a notation: *What about W/W? AG.*

What about Werewolf? Anthony Gibbs.

Cooling sat very still, like a meditating hermit, wrapped in the past, rooted in the present. He had come near to glimpsing what it was all about, yet now was the time when you had to tread warily. When evaluating a series of documents, one had to take the greatest care, remembering that you were always at the mercy of the person who had assembled the material. This was no random shuffle of classified reports. It had been put together with care—possibly by one person over a long period. The contents reflect a theory or, at worst, had been mustered to prove a theory. Cooling was almost certain of the answer to that final equation, but he was concerned, disturbed, by the reasoning behind the elaborate algebra.

Slowly he went on reading. The reports continued on Moonlight and Werewolf, but by the mid-sixties they had become almost casual sightings. As before, they did not form a pattern of constant surveillance. Seldom did the same operative file a report, yet things of importance were always noted.

There were three occasions when a whole flurry of reports erupted, like small explosions, in the files: a crisscross effect with Moonlight and Werewolf placed together with several other names. Meetings. Whole weeks or week-ends being spent with others, all of them slowing down, appearing, even in the terse reportage of classified intelligence, to be growing weary. All, that was, except Werewolf.

In the late sixties, Moonlight suffered a severe heart attack (again a meeting together of several names: coming to pay their respects). He lingered on while Werewolf went out and about, even travelled. Then, suddenly (Cooling felt a genuine shock), Moonlight died. Werewolf was on his own, and Cooling was more certain than ever of the thesis laid before him.

As the certainty bore in upon him he became more alert, and more sure that this rock of information was based on the sand of deception: either self-deception or the real thing. It was impossible to tell which. One fact could not be denied. Someone had gone to great lengths over the years to build up this strange fabrication—for there could be no truth in it.

Perhaps some gullible controller had latched on to a shred of misread evidence and provided the rest. Perhaps . . . ? He did not like to think of that possibility. Someone had taken it seriously, though? Why?

He covered the last twenty or thirty pages quickly, with mounting tension. They revealed one startling fact. Putting aside all the possible theories on the identity of Werewolf, Cooling now knew exactly where to find him. Maitland-Wood had wanted *him* to evaluate this collection of interrelated reports because he was familiar with modern German history and politics, and because he was a current specialist. There was another reason, though. As he came to the final pages, Cooling realised that he, and maybe he alone, was in a unique position. He could get close to Werewolf—whoever he was.

He had been chosen not simply because of his skill as an evaluator, but because through him there would be easy access to Werewolf.

He leaned back, dismissing his conclusions regarding Werewolf (for the third time in as many seconds) as preposterous. Surely nobody could really believe it? Werewolf, the inheritor of the Reich, the next in line within the Nazi Apostolic succession? The whole idea was both absurd and obscene. The raising of a ghost, separated from reality by thirty years of history during which judgement had been passed. Why now? The answer to that was because he was here and now. But what harm could it do? What harm now?

Tomorrow, he presumed, the Deputy Director would tell him. Not a big secret after all, only a small oddity, a strange warped fairy tale.

He scribbled his initials in the prescribed place and closed the whole bulky collection with a slam.

Tony Gibbs stirred. "Finished?" he asked.

Cooling nodded and looked at his watch. It was almost twenty minutes past two in the morning, and in his head the unclear figures of Moonlight and Werewolf picked their way through the Reich Chancellery garden, lit by the flash of shells, accompanied by the hell music of Berlin's passion, their noses assaulted by the stench of burning flesh. Behind them in the bunker, Joseph Goebbels and his sad, fanatic wife prepared for death among the corpses of those who had already died. And . . . ?

6

Sybil heard the raised voices as soon as she stepped
onto the landing. She had wakened with a start, turned
her head on the pillow and, blinking sleep from her
eyes, saw that it was a minute or so after eight o'clock.
Joseph was not in his familiar place beside her, though
the bed was still warm. In this first moment of con-
sciousness, Sybil became aware that he had only recently left her side.

He was not going back to London, to his office, until
after Christmas; that was part of the arrangement between them. But it was unusual, on any day, for him to
be first out of bed. Normally they both waited for Marina, the Portuguese girl, to bring them tea. Vaguely
she sensed something wrong; something disturbing the
harmony. Then she remembered the drawing on the

morning-room wall, and the way it had left her troubled. So much so that sleep had not come with its accustomed ease.

Still not fully awake, she came out onto the landing,
fastening her housecoat, shuffling slightly in her fluffy
mules. Far away below, in the kitchen, she thought,
Helen was being fractious, the little high whining voice
slightly overshadowed by the reasoned tones of Marina, who spoke good English, loved the child, and was
blessed with infinite patience. In the foreground were
the voices of the men. Joseph, not angry but firm, imi-
tated in dialogue with the deeper gruff of Hodge, the
builder and decorator.

Sybil began to make her way down the stairs.

"I know it will be covered by the wallpaper. That is
not the point, Mr. Hodge. It is a wasting of time for
one of your men to be making drawings on the wall.
I'm not fussing, but I am complaining. If a man has
time to make drawings like this, then he has time to be
getting on with work."

"And I'm telling you, Mr. Gotterson, that if these
lads tell me they haven't done the drawing, I accept
their word. None of these lads drew on the wall."

She reached the bottom of the stairs and could see
into the morning room: Joseph, in dressing gown and
slippers, his hair untidy, standing to face the window,
below which the drawing of the inverted eagle appeared, by daylight, even larger, more the work of a
wild, frustrated talent. Hodge, with the erect stance of

a retired soldier, was on Joseph's left, his three workmen ranged to the right as though posed for a photograph.

Though Hodge had referred to them as "lads," only
one of the trio qualified for that category. Paul, the
thin, gangling apprentice with long, fair hair falling to
his shoulders and often across his face, which was pale
and pinched, the eyes permanently undersmudged by
dark circles which spoke of nights spent—Charlie the
carpenter maintained—up to no good with Veronica, a
well-known young woman in the village.

Charlie the carpenter was an old craftsman, short,
grizzled, smelling of wood chippings, his lined face
reflecting the sad knowledge that he was one of a
dying breed. The third artisan, Tom the painter and
plasterer, a dark, proud man in his mid-forties, carried
himself with the careful assurance of one who has
reached his zenith—wife, children, home, a little care
and no more ambition than to do his best work wherever Hodge sent him.

"Anyway, none of these lads could draw anything
like that. It's a fair bit artistic." Hodge closed his mouth
at the end of the sentence as though this was the final
word on the subject.

"It's repellent."

"Well, sir," Hodge's voice took on a patient tone.
"They say they found it yesterday afternoon when they
stripped the last piece of wallpaper from under the
window. I believe them."

"I did not see it yesterday afternoon."

"Well, you wouldn't have done." It was young Paul, the most likely suspect, speaking up. "You come in here about half-past four yesterday afternoon, just afore we packed up. You didn't come in again till late on."

"I came in late afternoon, yes, and I did not see it. I saw it late last night. My wife called me and . . ."

"Well, you wouldn't have seen it at half four. I was here. Remember? I was finishing off that bit of skirting down by the fireplace. The bit Charlie put in yesterday morning. I moved the pasting table out of the way. I moved it in front of the window. It had the dust cloths hanging round it. You wouldn't have seen the drawing through them: not at half-past four."

"Morning, Mrs. Gotterson." Hodge turned, catching sight of Sybil in the doorway. "We're trying to sort out the matter of this drawing here. I'm attempting to convince Mr. Gotterson that none of these lads had a hand in it."

Sybil was trying to accurately recall the time she had last been in the room on the previous day: apart from late, when she had first seen the drawing. She remembered that it was sometime in the afternoon. Charlie had been doing the skirting board in the morning, she had seen that. Yes, in the afternoon Tom and the boy had been working under the window, possibly stripping the paper away.

"We did not see it until last night. Late." Joseph stubborn and unconvinced.

"It wasn't there to be seen, sir." Tom spoke for the first time. "The drawing was under the wallpaper. Then the paste table was in front of it. In any case you can see it's not done recent. It's not new. That's obvious."

"Not to me."

Charlie sighed. "It's a pity I didn't mention it to you. I was in a mind to, but you were in the studio when we packed up: the study as you call it." Then, almost as an afterthought, "You know it's the second we've come across?"

"The second?" Sybil advanced towards the drawing, peering forward to examine it again, then straightening. Through the window she could see the six tall Wellingtonias which fronted the house, just within the grey wall. Above the wall, over the road, the eaves and upper windows of a large neighbouring house were visible.

"Before you arrived," Charlie went on. "In the studio. Only that one was the right way around. They'd be the work of Miss Ayerton's niece, Martha, the one whose child was . . ." He stopped abruptly, looking towards Hodge, who had begun to speak, cutting in on him.

"Miss Ayerton had a niece who painted. That's why the studio was built. Miss Ayerton built it for her. Some folks reckoned that Miss Ayerton painted, but she didn't."

"I can remember it being built," said Charlie. "So can you, Mr. Hodge, your old man built it."

Miss Ayerton was the last resident of Pine Copse End: the granddaughter of the man who had erected the house. It had been in the one family only, and Miss Ayerton was well known and remembered in the village. In her final years she had lived the life of a recluse, dying at a great age only a few years ago.

"So the niece liked drawing eagles." Joseph sounded almost mocking, as though this had some great significance.

"Eagles?" Charlie grinned, shifting his feet. "Beggin' your pardon, Mr. Gotterson, but that's no eagle, that's a sparrow hawk. A big bugger an' all. It was a sparrow hawk as killed the . . ."

"Come on, Charlie, there's no point in going over old stories." Hodge's brow creased into a scowl of disapproval. He spoke very fast.

"Killed what?" asked Sybil, an involuntary cold shiver tracing, like a small barb of ice, up her spine.

"It's old history, Mrs. Gotterson, old history. And it's unpleasant. It shouldn't bear the telling. Let it die."

"But it is history and this lady and gentlemen're living in the house." Charlie took a couple of paces back and appeared to be examining the skirting board again. He did not look at them when he spoke. "They should hear, Mr. Hodge. It happened. The village'll never forget it happening. God, you even remember it, as I do. Lads we were."

"What's all this about?" Joseph looked at Sybil, a questioning worry in his face, like a man suspecting tragic news.

Hodge gave a deep sigh of capitulation. "Well, I should've thought you'd have heard it before now. Should've thought the agent ud've told you. But then again I suppose there's no need." He rummaged in his pocket, bringing out a battered packet of cigarettes. "You mind if I smoke?"

"I don't wish to stop you." Joseph was always prim over the matter of nicotine: as though smoking was the breaking of some religious rule which he held sacred.

They had unconsciously formed a circle around Hodge; and so the story came out, in daylight as it had happened, and all the more horrible because of that.

Pine Copse End had been built by Miss Ayerton's grandfather, the foundations going down about 1854. But the old man did not live to see the house completed. It stood half finished for a few years until his son eventually took over and the whole family, father, mother and the daughter, Alice—the famed Miss Ayerton—moved in towards the end of the 1870s. Three or four years later the mother died giving birth (in the house) to a son.

The boy, Harold, eventually died on the Somme in the first great war to end all wars, leaving behind a wife and one child: a girl, Martha. Miss Ayerton's father died (also in the house) towards the end of 1919, she must, Hodge said, have been in her mid-forties then, for it was generally thought that she was in her late nineties at the time of her death.

It seemed that she was the only really fortunate member of the Ayerton family, for her brother's widow was killed in a street accident in the early twenties, leaving the girl, Martha, then about seventeen or eighteen years of age.

Miss Alice Ayerton, who had stayed on at Pine Copse End, was looked after by a companion-cum-housekeeper, and an old gardener—Bob Hallet, a local man who had actually gone on working at the house until well into the 1940s.

"She took her niece in and looked after her like a mother," Hodge told them. "But somehow the girl was a wild one. Oh, she was talented enough; could paint and draw. Even had some pictures exhibited in London, I believe. And there's one or two here in the village. Miss Alice had the studio built for her, as Charlie says, by my father. I think the girl had ideas of becoming a great artist."

"Bohemian," added Charlie.

"Well," shrugged Hodge, "maybe she was; or maybe she was just a bit fey. Used to spend a lot of time up there in the copse, and in the woods, drawing and sketching." There was a pause, as though he was loath to go on. Then—"They never knew who the man was."

"Some had a good idea." Charlie gave a twisted smile, one hard hand to his chin.

"Maybe they did. Anyway, it wasn't long before the whole village knew what had become of Miss Martha Ayerton. The old lady stood by her though, I'll say that. There was no sweeping it away under the carpet like some people did in those days. It wasn't like it is nowadays. She was having a baby out of wedlock, and Miss Ayerton wasn't one for dodging the issue. The child was born here as well. Right here in the house. I somehow think old Miss Ayerton felt it was like getting something back—her mother and father having died in the house, like. I remember seeing the kid myself. Young Martha couldn't have been more than twenty-three, twenty-four years old. I can see her now, wheeling him through the village. Lovely baby. I remember him plain. Mind you, some people didn't like it; crossed over on the other side, if you follow my meaning. He's buried up in the churchyard. There's a stone to him; you can see it: up the top by the trees. William Walter Ayerton."

"What . . . ?" It stuck in Sybil's throat, for there was a brooding sense of tragedy about the story which seemed to fill the room. Tom and young Paul obviously knew it all, but they stood stock still, faces impassive, as though waiting for the inevitable. Joseph moved closer to her.

"Funny creatures, birds," muttered Charlie. "You ever see that film, *The Birds?* Where all the birds attack this village? It's really happened a few times, you know."

"Yes, I've seen it on television," whispered Sybil.

"No." Joseph shook his head.

"He'd be about eighteen months old," Hodge continued. "He was toddling anyhow—you can work out his age from the gravestone. Summer's morning, out there on the lawn." He inclined his head towards the back of the house. "He was toddling around, playing with a ball. His mother used to sit out there looking after him, and drawing and sketching. She popped into the house for something—a new pencil or something I believe it was. Just for a minute, like. No harm. Bob, the gardener, wasn't far away. I heard him tell it a dozen times." He took a deep breath and coughed. "I think he and young Martha both heard the screams about the same time. Bob Hallet was in the potting shed and he ran out real quick. Damn great sparrow hawk, it was. Huge, he said. It'd be a female, they're always the bigger and most aggressive. No reason to it. Just came down and attacked the child. Bob tried to get to him, but the bird kept on coming, striking with her beak. Then Bob got a stick, and he finally drove it off. But it was too late, you see. Ripped at the little chap's throat and in his neck and eyes. They got him down the hospital, but it was too late." He shook his head sadly. "Too late. Lost too much blood. They think they shot the bird about a week later. It'd been going for some chickens. I know everyone was terrified after it happened. I was scared stiff."

"Oh God." Sybil felt sick and shocked by the idea: the picture that Hodge had conjured. On their lawn; outside their drawing room; below their bedroom: the child screaming and the bird striking again and again; the blood and the feathers. Then the mother and the moment of panic.

"How terrible." Joseph put his arm around her. "Terrible," he repeated.

"I think young Martha went a bit funny after that." Hodge appeared more relaxed, as though he was pleased to be done with the worst part of the tale. "She left the village a year or so later. She used to draw that damned bird all over the place."

Sybil could not take her eyes from the drawing, while in her head she heard the beat of wings, just as she had heard them from the bedroom window.

"Some say that Miss Ayerton had her put away." Charlie cocked his head, his expression saying that he knew more than he was prepared to tell.

"What a horrible . . ." Sybil began to speak, then stopped as they heard little Helen's voice rise from the kitchen, then the scamper of her feet as she ran into the hall and towards the room calling excitedly, "Mummy, Mummy, Mummy," bubbling, ready to greet her parents.

Sybil turned, half knelt with her arms outstretched as the child propelled herself into the room, fresh-cheeked, a flurry of arms and legs, her blond hair flying: showing off in a wild and silly mood.

Sybil grabbed her, hugging close as if to protect her from the remnants of the story which clung to her imagination. "Hallo, darling. Golly, you're heavy. What'd you have for breakfast?"

Marina stood in the doorway, mouthing apologies at having let the child loose.

Helen tugged herself away, shouting in a sing-song, "Mummy, where's the baby? Where's the baby, Mummy? The baby?"

"Don't be silly, darling. What baby?"

"The baby, Mummy. The baby what was crying. In the night it woke me up. The baby?" Her giggle of laughter which followed did nothing to warm the sudden chill which seemed to envelop all of them.

7

Cooling often wondered if his detached interest in war had something to do with his date of birth. Child psychiatrists pontificate about the first few years of one's life, pointing to circumstances and conditions as the mainspring of future characteristics. To have been born during the closing months of 1938, living out one's first years against a background of death, deprivation and destruction, could well, he thought, be the reason why he was at his best when dealing with matters of military violence in the abstract.

Both his father and mother had been intelligent people, who, under normal circumstances, might possibly have allowed themselves the uncertain luxury of a long engagement. As things turned out they met in the late summer of 1937—he a hard little Yorkshire garage owner, she a shy Wimbledon flower. They were married by Christmas. Two years after Cooling was born, his father was blown to pieces in the rear turret of a Whitley bomber over the North Sea. His mother had never thought about remarriage, and young Vincent, the computer of his mind probably full of half-digested wartime incidents, had gone from school to university with an intense interest in the cut and thrust of large-scale strategy and tactics, all watched from afar. Never once had he felt the desire to come up against the realities of war—cold or hot—in any personal or physical way.

It was an attitude which created curiosity among his superiors in the security service. Cooling, they all agreed, was a cold fish. His name even seemed to be a reflection of his attitude, and they were also quick to note that, while he remained determined not to be caught up in active work on the clandestine side, his evaluations, which so often concerned the more violent aspects of the secret world, were always logical and aloof. He was, they considered, the kind of man who would approach the strategy of nuclear war with the coldness of a chess champion.

Those who had taken the trouble to examine Cooling's complex psychology in detail were also aware that, in a strangely paradoxical way, he outwardly despised the tools of war—and in the trade this included those personalities who worked on the clandestine side.

Tony Gibbs, who knew of this better than any other man, had made it quite plain to the Deputy Director; so, before Cooling even set eyes on the file, they had been reasonably certain of his initial reaction.

When Cooling left the study to climb upstairs to his secure bedroom, Tony Gibbs crossed to the door, locked it, picked up the file and went over to the bookcase. Cooling had been right about the depth of that piece of furniture, though wrong about what it contained. There was no radio housing, or even a radio, in the room, for the bookcase simply contained a metal fireproof safe. With the file locked away, Gibbs returned to the desk and picked up the small interhouse telephone. In the master bedroom, as they all jocularly called it, a small red light began to wink on the instrument next to Maitland-Wood's bed.

"He's finished it. All closed down for the night," said Gibbs.

"Reaction?" asked the Deputy Director, pen poised over a document lying, on his brief case, across his thighs. He shifted slightly against the pillows arranged behind him.

"No questions. He behaved like a gentleman. But everything else was much as we thought. He appeared put out: interested in a professional way, but slightly ruffled."

Maitland-Wood grunted. "He's wondering why. Very well, Tony, I'll tell him in the morning. As we arranged."

93

One of the elderly house slaves brought tea to Cooling just after eight. On the tray was a small, unmarked envelope.

"Breakfast between nine and ten," said the slave, retreating with a nod.

Cooling wondered who else he had served with dinner, early morning tea and breakfast in this house. Some of them, he considered, would almost certainly have been very frightened people.

There were two lines written in longhand on the paper which he pulled from the envelope:

We have a silent breakfast here. The Deputy Director will see you in the study at ten-fifteen. AG.

To set the next piece of homework, no doubt, he thought. You should now know who Werewolf is and where he's at. Go and sort him out.

He sipped his tea, got out of bed, performed his ablutions, dressed and went downstairs.

Both Maitland-Wood and Gibbs were already at the table, each with a pile of newspapers. They looked up and nodded at Cooling's arrival, returning to their reading with almost studied indifference. It was all very Old World: the line of silver dishes on the sideboard, the padding slaves filling the coffee cups and replenishing the toast racks. At the end of the sideboard a little pile of newspapers. In Berlin his first duty of the day was to make a quick scan of all the British, American and German papers—Hardwicke did the Russian; Nash and Horsefield covered the remainder. It was a chore he could do without today. His hand hovered over *The Times* and then moved swiftly to the *Mail*.

As he reached his chair, clutching a plate of bacon, sausage and eggs, one of the slaves homed in like a fighter, whispering, "Black or white, sir?" the silver pot poised over the cup. The silence was strangely monastic, in itself at odds with the clubland surrounding, and, as time progressed, Cooling was surprised when Gibbs winked heavily at him on leaving the table. A daring gesture, he considered.

At ten-fifteen he tapped on the study door. The Deputy Director was alone behind the desk, head down over a pile of flimsies. They had probably been brought up from the Ministry, he thought, conscious of having heard the front door bell ring during breakfast.

Maitland-Wood smiled and waved Cooling into a chair then went back to the paper before him. He looked at it for a moment, then, with some precision, capped his pen, replaced it in his pocket and stretched.

"Good to see you. You examined the file?"

Cooling nodded.

"And?"

"You want an evaluation now?"

"Evaluation and the prescription."

He shook his had. "No action. Evaluation, on this evidence: exceptional long-term surveillance; no conclusions."

"Why not?"

"Not enough information. Not enough strong indicators. No convincing arguments for action to be taken."

The Deputy Director smiled, almost a grin, "Good." He spoke like a man who has just heard about the demise of his greatest enemy. "What would you need in order to offer a full evaluation?"

"Time to go back over everything—the documents; a certain amount of precision regarding who's who."

"And who do you think is who?" the question hanging like a small threat.

"We're talking about Moonlight and Werewolf? Mainly Werewolf?"

"Naturally."

"I have no idea about Moonlight, except he is supposed to be an SS Sturmbannführer. As for Werewolf, I know who I am supposed to think he is."

The Deputy Director sucked his teeth. "But you have to be convinced?"

"As you say, I have to be convinced. Can I ask questions?"

Maitland-Wood nodded slowly, like a toy Alsatian in the back of a car.

"Who assembled the file?"

A pause, more for effect than thought. "I did."

"So I would assume that you are a believer?"

"That's why you're here. I also need convincing on the question of Werewolf's identity. But that's not the major problem. I think it really depends on who Werewolf himself thinks he is."

Cooling shuffled his feet, then, as though coming to a firm decision, crossed his legs. "But you have a preference?"

"Haven't you?"

"Yes. I think it's a load of rubbish: a bit of melodrama. I also think it's very bad evaluation so far. As I said, the long-term surveillance has been very good, but all the other stuff . . ." He shrugged.

"You mean Werewolf being the boy emperor? The heir apparent? The natural inheritor of Hitler's spoiled kingdom?"

Cooling nodded again. "Rubbish," he said firmly. "The whole concept is against the evidence as I remember it. And it's based on a story told by your subject Shallow in 1947, and the secondhand memory of a braggart who might have been one of the elite bodyguards. There's nothing more than that. Rumours, gossip. They come from a hundred-odd stories about the last days. No more substance than mist or ghosts."

Maitland-Wood smiled reflectively. "There is the surveillance. There is the fact of Moonlight and Werewolf."

"The boy emperor in hiding, being trained to take over his future kingdom?"

"Moonlight was a fact. Werewolf *is* a fact. Moreover he is here, and he is now. He is also accessible. Maybe you should know more. There is positive identification on Moonlight. There is documentation . . ."

"Then why isn't it included in the file?"

"My decision," the Deputy Director snapped.

"Leading me through the maze?"

"Something like that. But he certainly existed, and we are ninety-nine per cent certain that he left the bunker with Werewolf on the night of May 1, 1945."

"Though it's only fifty-fifty on who Werewolf is?"

"True, but there is something else. You say the surveillance is exceptional. You are wrong. It is good, but there's something else not in the file. He made frequent journeys abroad at the end of the sixties, right?"

"They seemed well covered."

"Not altogether. On one of those trips he was able to establish residency in England. We boobed, missed it. Now it's too late, and has been for a while. He's a British citizen: naturalised."

"Does it matter that much?"

"The Minister seems to think it does."

"In case it gets blown, spread all over the newspapers?"

"It is seen as something possibly more sinister than that. I'll admit that evidence, as it stands, is pretty inconclusive—I was Cobra by the way. I opened the file in the first place, so I have a vested interest."

"I said you were a believer."

"And I said that what really matters is who Were-wolf thinks he is. If he is a believer, as you put it."

"I don't think it has any relevance, sir. I don't honestly think it matters."

"Well, the crystal-gazers would disagree. They see two, at the most three, possible scenarios for this country in the next decade. One, that under the present conditions it will collapse economically and possibly descend to the same level as Germany between the wars. Two, that the political Ping-pong match for power will go on, with the spoils eventually going to whichever party becomes the strongest. Three, and this is the natural outcome of either of the first two possibilities, there will be a massive confrontation between extreme left and extreme right bringing about a polarisation—the silent "don't knows" making up their minds at last, and a split right down the centre: no middle way."

Cooling stared at the ceiling. "So whatever happens the right wing would claim Werewolf. You really think that the collective memory is that short?"

"No, but I believe that the more one party is pushed towards the Communist ideal, however shrouded in socialist doctrine, the more likely it is that the right wing will accept the possibility of a kind of national socialism: national socialism without the fanatical extremes of racialism which Germany had under Hitler. They'll go for law and order . . ."

"And the trains running on time?"

"It could be that simple. Muzzle the unions, give wider power to the police, reunite the country under a national chauvinist banner. Stern times, stern measures."

"Heil, Werewolf."

"Maybe." He barked the word as though convinced.

"And maybe Stalin isn't dead either. Perhaps the left will resurrect him. Come on, sir, it's paranoid."

The Deputy Director nodded. "Absolutely. But it is a fact that Werewolf has our lords and masters in a sweat. They do not like his presence here."

"Deport him, then. Shove him in jail. Your people have the ways and means, sir. The ways and means, and that coy jargon they use. Can't you sanctify him, or give him a dose of measles? Isn't that how your people talk about blackmail and murder?"

"Exactly how they talk. But Werewolf has an English wife with English relatives. He also has an English child. The Minister insists that we are to do nothing which might leave us open to scandal. The security services do seem to be prime targets these days."

"You can't give him measles in case somebody cocks it up and it all gets into the papers; or in case some civil rights people start shouting."

"He must be persuaded to go of his own volition. We must persuade him, and the decision has to be his."

"And what am I supposed to do about it?"

"In the end you will have the cleanest access. My dear Cooling," he said, smiling, a vulpine leer. "I didn't have you pulled out of Berlin just for your good looks and ability. The fact that your mother is living but a stone's throw from our subject played a large part in that decision." His jaws snapped shut, the smile gone. "But, to start with, I want a proper evaluation. After that we have to find out exactly who he believes he is."

"Or who he knows he is."

Maitland-Wood looked down his nose. "That's more complex and you damn well know it, Vincent. If he's simply the boy whom Hitler decorated for knocking out a Russian tank, the knowledge of his identity could well be deeply buried in his subconscious." He lifted a hand, held it, palm down, for a second and brought it slowly towards the desk. "What I need from you is a scientific evaluation: a total weighing up of the possibilities. I want you to prove, or disapprove, to me the feasibility of the substitution theory; give me an analysis; show me who might have set it up and how. Whether it is plausible. That would be your first stage. How long would it take?"

"Depends on the facilities."

"You'll have a free run of the archives. We'll bring whatever you need from the Ministry into our own registry. All documents."

"And all the names? The Director's *Black Book D.*"

Maitland-Wood hesitated.

"Don't you have the final say?" asked Vincent. Was the Deputy Director perhaps pursuing a private project? Building his own empire. It was not unknown in the politics of the trade.

"If you need it, you'll see the *Black Book D.*" He frowned.

"Where shall I live?"

"Here?"

"With your squads on my back?"

"Just watching your back. You'll be free to come and go as you please. How long?"

"Couple of weeks. A month perhaps. I shall want some free time—like Christmas."

"I was going to suggest you spend Christmas with your mother in any case."

Cooling sighed. They had you all ways. He bit back on the anger. Christmas with his mother. The true reason for him being chosen. Access to Werewolf through his mother. Within spitting distance.

"You might as well," the Deputy Director said, smirking: a man who knew he held a royal flush. "After the evaluation you'll want to get in close anyway. Stage two: find out who he believes he is."

"You want him run out of the country with the hounds of hell on his tail, but no comeback and no fuss. That's not my kind of work, sir."

"You'll have help. You'll have a squad. We've already put a wireman on the phones. It'll be a team effort, Vincent."

"Play up, play up and play the game."

"Why not?"

Cooling stared into space. Again he saw the SS officer leading the small boy over the rubble, against the burning sky, out of the Führer-bunker thirty years ago. A small boy? Some small boys had been brought to the bunker on April 20, 1945, to be decorated by the Führer. Ten days later Hitler lay dead with Eva Braun; the day after that Hitler's most loyal partner, Joseph Goebbels, committed suicide with his wife, Magda, in the Chancellery garden. Inside the bunker his children lay murdered. Six of them: five girls and a boy.

It was mad, fantastic, preposterous. It made no sense of the facts. Yet, Maitland-Wood insisted, the boy who had left the bunker on that night was now in England, living under cover as an Englishman. The department believed it.

"I'll do the first stage at least, sir," he said, disgusted with himself, because he knew how far it would involve him.

"I thought you might." The Deputy Director shuffled his papers together briskly. "Tony Gibbs'll make all the arrangements. This is serious, you know. Our subject's contacts in Denmark and Sweden are high-grade neo-Nazis. There's no doubt about that, and the movement flourishes. Here? Well, he has been approached by Column 88—and don't laugh at Column 88. They sow the seeds of threat." He paused, one hand sweeping over his hair. "Report to me. Where do you propose to start?"

"With you, sir. I'll start with Cobra." Cooling leaned forward.

8

When Willis Maitland-Wood was called home from Vienna in August of 1939, he left behind him three deeply planted networks comprising some fourteen agents. In the department, they became known as the Driftwood Grid, and during the next four years their yield varied between high and medium-grade intelligence. In February of 1944 all but one went dead, and Maitland-Wood did not re-establish contact with members of this remaining group until late in 1946.

In the years between, he had, as people said at the time, a good war. He shuttled between the department and Special Operations Executive, ran the Driftwood Grid long-range, and was personally responsible for putting twenty agents into occupied Europe. When the war ended, he was thirty years old and a small departmental legend. In the immediate months which followed, most of his time was taken up tracing his people in France and Norway, so it was not until late in 1946 that he was able to return to Austria and run a terminal trace on the Driftwood Grid.

As he admitted to Cooling, it was difficult. The occupation zones presented a problem, while the name of the game was rapidly altering, shifting perspective. For instance, he was not surprised to learn that one of his networks was intact but working for the Russians, as it had been since '44. The second had been partially blown, while three agents of the third had disappeared without leaving a ripple.

"Our own people, particularly the Field Security boys, were sympathetic to the DPs, but in a position of compromise. Palestine was a thorn in the flesh, you know."

The Deputy Director had settled into his story, telling it straight, like someone chatting out his war memoirs. Cooling could not be anything but impressed at the man's memory, for he filled everything with small detail and colour, making it live as though it had happened yesterday.

"The Austrian authorities weren't any help either. I felt sorry for the FSS. There was pressure from all sides: watch the Jews, watch the possible political people co-operate on catching war criminals. Each of those instructions was at variance with the others. Anyway, I was under military cover, combing the DP camps for traces of my people. That was how I came to be sharing an office with FSS at Admont. I'd had Christmas at home and got back there around the second of January, forty-seven. It was bloody bleak. I'd had indicators that two of my fellows had been in the hands of the Gestapo in Vienna, and there were half a dozen men in the Admont DP camp who'd shared that dubious privilege. I'd been there two days when the FSS brought in Shallow.

"During the morning a couple of Poles came in and made statements concerning a man they'd seen, over the Christmas period, working on a farm nearby. They were both ex-Dachau and made quite a fuss: a little chap with a limp and a tall scarecrow fellow who said he'd been a doctor. I think the FSS would have preferred to sidestep the issue, but in the end they went off and brought the German in."

"His real name?" Cooling asked.

"You won't have to cross-reference, you'll have his file with the others. He was called Schmidt, like ten thousand others. Clemens Schmidt. There was no doubt, from the word go, that he'd been at Dachau. The Poles recognised him. He recognised them." He gave a dry laugh. "Old home week. They accused him of nothing—you've seen it in the file—they knew he had witnessed a number of unpleasant incidents, but he admitted none of that. Administrative quill-driver: even had all his papers to prove it, pay book, the lot."

"What was he like under interrogation?"

"What were any of them like? Anxious to help. He was quite a pleasant fellow really. Big; big hands. A kind of gentle giant. I got the impression that he obeyed orders well. Good NCO, but wasn't going to land any of his former colleagues in it."

"His story about being on special detachment to Berlin: was that substantiated?"

The Deputy Director nodded. "Absolutely. He'd been moved back like everybody. He was in Berlin for Christmas forty-four. With friend Moonlight from January."

"What about Moonlight?"

"Identity? You won't need the Director's *Black Book* for that either. He's cross-referenced as well, though you won't have heard of him. There's a file as long as your arm. I instituted that."

"Name?"

"Kritter. Max Kritter. Read it for yourself."

"Give me a line drawing."

"Born 1902, Stuttgart. Member of the Leibstandarte SS Adolf Hitler at its inception in 1933. Later transferred many times. Fanatical loyalty to the Führer. Bypassed Himmler and all that mystical rubbish that seemed so important to him. You'll find evidence that his loyalty was rather special: that he even allowed himself to be passed over for promotion in order to serve Hitler. It would seem that he, in fact, took his personal orders from the horse's mouth. It's all there, constant transfers; pops up in the most unlikely places;

the Chancellery, Berchtesgaden, Rastenburg, Bad Nau-
heim. The inferences are that he watched the
watchers."

"What was this special detachment?"

"Winkling out army dissidents, and God knows there
were plenty of them."

"What, a major and a couple of corporals?"

"A couple of corporals who obeyed orders and kept
quiet."

"And you believed Schmidt's story about the
bunker?"

"It was almost an aside. He was trying to be helpful."

"And save his neck?"

"There was no question of saving his neck."

"But he could have been motivated into telling a
fiction, simply to be in the FSS's good books?"

"I think not. My impression was that he didn't have
a large imagination. He could obey orders; he was co-
operative; he didn't lie openly, and he didn't drop or
stop anyone in it."

"You believed him." Cooling pressed, stating it
baldly.

"He was there all right. He was around the bunker.
There was no doubt about that. The detail's too strong;
it matched up. Yes, I believed his story."

"Because you wanted to believe it?"

"I don't follow you."

"It was January forty-seven. Hitler's death was still
part of a myth; a legend. There were persistent ru-

mours, stories. He had escaped; the Russians had him; he was in South America; he was living with Eva in a castle in Spain."

"Those ghosts had already been laid. Most of them, anyway."

"You'd read Trevor-Roper's report by then?"

"Yes, I'd read it. It was available to the general public later in forty-seven."

"You'd read it and agreed with it?"

"In the main, yes."

"You didn't have any pet theories of your own?"

"I thought the Russians knew a great deal more than they were saying. As it happened, they did. No, I had no private theories. I was doing another kind of job. It wasn't my concern."

"Until Schmidt told his story about holding the Hitler Youth lad and seeing him leave the bunker with Moonlight—Kritter—on the night of first May. Were you conversant with the dates?"

"I knew that we were claiming Hitler's suicide on thirtieth April, the murder of the Goebbels children and Goebbels' suicide on first May, yes."

"And you put two and two together straight away? When you heard Schmidt's story?"

"It crossed my mind, no more than that. To be honest with you, Kritter interested me more than the boy. To start with, it was a hobby."

"Which became an obsession?"

"Far from it, Cooling. Have care, you're going to become offensive in a minute."

"I can't help that. I need to know why you took action."

"I didn't take action. A month or so later I was back in London. One of my duties was checking the trace reports on wanted Nazis. Kritter wasn't wanted but he had turned up, in Spain with the boy, May forty-five. I had Schmidt's story on file, under Shallow. The two married, so I instituted the file—trace and survey. No more than that."

The old man was getting spiky, you could tell it in the cutting edge of his voice. Enough was enough for one day.

"May I speak with you again when I've been through all the material?"

"Of course."

"And, sir," as casual as possible, "could you instruct Gibbs? You know what I need and it'll come better from you. I'll only come back and ask for more if I think there's anything missing."

Maitland-Wood gave a slow nod. "If there is anything missing, it's because we haven't got it."

Cooling was at the door before he asked, "Tomorrow be too soon for me to start?"

"Not at all. I'll see they give you your own reading room. Just let Gibbs know your movements—your rough movements, for the domestic side, housekeeping."

He thought he would give them a run for their money. The Deputy Director had said they would be watching his back, but he knew that covered a multitude of sins. Gibbs was in the drawing room, fidgeting.

"I'll be out most of the morning. In to lunch, but I'm not sure about dinner." Cooling was almost curt with him, and Gibbs looked hurt, as though he was being betrayed.

Half-way up the Haymarket he spotted two of them: one in front and one behind. They probably had a couple of cars as well, using him as a training exercise. He crossed Piccadilly and Regent Street, turning into the Regent Palace to use their pay phones. It was not the best way, but at least he could see who was in the next booth. In any case, there were only two numbers he wanted to call and they probably had both of them wired.

He telephoned his mother first and told her he would be down on Christmas Eve. She was delighted and asked no questions. As he dialled the number of Steph's firm's London office, he wondered if they had completely wired his mother's flat.

Steph was in New York with her boss and not expected back until tomorrow. Would she be in the office tomorrow? Yes, they thought she would, and could they tell her who had called? Just a friend, he said, and rang off. The man in the next booth was short and wore an expensive overcoat; he reeled off a list of figures from a little notebook. Cooling would have bet a month's salary that he was talking to the Speaking Clock.

He went up Piccadilly, crossed over and had coffee at Fortnum and Mason's, then retraced his footsteps and headed towards Leicester Square and the book-shops of the Charing Cross Road, his mind partly on the team that moved around him, and partly on Steph.

They had met a year ago at Hardwicke's place: the pre-Christmas party with Hardwicke's fluffy little wife twittering and showing too much cleavage. At the time, they both wondered if Hardwicke had been matchmaking—she had known the Hardwickes for a long time and they were always telling her that she ought to get married. He saw her again on New Year's Eve and they brought in 1975 together in his small bed, with the stereo playing something schmaltzy, like the Sibelius violin concerto. After that it was once or twice a week: dinner, drinks, sometimes a film or concert, usually bed. They spoke only of neutral things and she did not pry—he presumed that she had an ink-ling of Hardwicke's work, so knew that he was in the same line of business. Never once did she suggest that there was anything more than a close open relationship. No strings. No future. Rarely did she express enjoy-ment in their sex, and it was only after she had left Berlin that he realised how much he missed her.

"No sad goodbyes," she had said when they parted. "It's not like that, is it?"

He agreed that it wasn't and kept a firm control over the letters he wrote to her. It would be unnatural for him not to wonder, now, what it would be like meeting her again, in London.

Standing outside one of the second-hand bookshops, Cooling felt suddenly very alone, on the brink of this journey which might fuse past and present into some ludicrous whole. He thought about his mother, and the village of Tilt.

He had to try four shops before he collected all the books: Trevor-Roper's *Last Days of Hitler*, a couple of books on Goebbels, and Alan Bullock's definitive *Hitler, A Study in Tyranny*. Then he went back to St. James's to eat chicken Kiev with Gibbs; the two of them alone in the splendid little dining room being served by the slaves with Mid-European accents. In the afternoon he did his homework before starting the long haul through the past as it was interpreted in the department files.

9

The first incident concerning the sugar occurred four days before Christmas, though at the time Sybil hardly noticed it, thinking that she had probably made a mistake. After all, what with the decorators, and preparations for their first Christmas in the new house, it was not surprising that she overlooked some things. She certainly did not connect it with the noises in the night.

The evening routine of the Gotterson household ran to a loosely set pattern. Of course timing varied, depending on what they were doing. It was Sunday night. Helen was bathed and put to bed, as usual, around six o'clock. Joseph went up and read her a story, and they both sat with her for a little time before Marina tucked her in for the night.

They had a cold meal just after seven-thirty. Marina

ate with them and spent the remainder of the evening in the kitchen. She had a portable television and was quite happy watching it while she caught up on a few chores: some washing for Helen, and a bit of mending before doing the vegetables for the following day.

Joseph announced that he had a lot of letters to finish, and retired into the study. Sybil, who had been fairly energetic during the afternoon—taking Helen for a walk and running around with her in the over-grown garden—curled up on the sofa in the drawing room. The television was switched on, though the pro-grammes were far from compulsive, so it was not sur-prising that, when Marina looked in to say good night around ten-thirty, she was dozing.

She shook herself awake and stretched, feeling that she knew the luxury dogs must feel after sleeping by a fireside. Then she went through to the study, where Joseph was still writing, the stereo system turned up to full blast: Berlioz, *Symphonie Fantastique.*

He told her that he would be finished and ready for bed in about ten minutes.

"Usual drink?" she asked.

"Of course, Angel."

He looked up, smiling, rubbing his back against the chair like an animal. She considered that she was obsessed with domestic pets tonight, but it was a sen-sual movement. She knew that look and smile. It would not be straight to sleep tonight.

The milky drink habit had started soon after they

had settled in London, yet she always asked him, taking nothing for granted as far as Joseph was concerned. This little nightly exchange had become a kind of ritual which served other purposes, like private sexual signals. They never discussed it, though each of them had become aware of the other's needs transmitted in this almost obligatory routine.

In the kitchen she took down the tin of cocoa, measured out the milk and set it on the stove, going through these accustomed automatic actions with her mind upon her husband and the private wonder she constantly nursed.

Before the shy, hesitant Joseph had come into her life, there had been many men: a couple of intense relationships and quite a few casual affairs. In those days, during moments of intimate confessions shared with other girls, she had often affirmed that she could never become a one-man girl. Joseph had changed that, and it was a regular source of amazement to her that, as far as the physical side of marriage was concerned, she had thrived on him instead of becoming bored like she had so often done in the past.

Reaching for the sugar bowl—they shared a liking for sweet things—she experienced a mild irritation on discovering that it was less than a third full. Why was it that the sugar bowl always needed filling when *she* wanted to use it? Her hand was on the store cupboard door when she realised that they were quite out of sugar. Marina had opened the last bag yesterday morning. She had made a mental note to get some in the village, but for some reason it had gone right out of her mind.

She swore softly to herself, opening the cupboard to make absolutely certain there was not a spare bag tucked away. No, the only sugar in the house was the miserable amount in the bowl. Well, there was enough for tonight, and probably enough for Marina to use first thing in the morning. The girl would just have to nip along to the village with Helen and get some before she brought their tea to them in bed.

She went through the bare, uncarpeted hall and brought back the telephone message pad, which lay on the boards next to the instrument by the bottom of the stairs.

Leaving the note propped up near the stove, where Marina would see it, she made the cocoa and carried it upstairs.

As it happened the cocoa remained untouched.

"Making love to you," Joseph whispered later, "is always refreshing. It is like diving into a deep pond and then coming up into the sunlight."

He was not the most subtle man with romantic compliments, but all the same Sybil drifted into sleep content, warm and with great peace of mind.

She woke with a start, knowing that it was still the middle of the night and wondering if she had been dreaming. For the first few seconds she was confused and unable to tell whether the sounds were part of a dream or something real which had disturbed her.

She eased herself up in bed, trying to peer through the darkness, ears straining to catch the sounds still in her mind. Joseph was silent, deeply asleep beside her, and she was conscious of her own heartbeat. It must have been a dream: the sequence of sounds were too clear and distinct, like an echo in her brain: the scuffle of feet and what could have been a giggle. There was silence now, the night stillness within the house and, outside, around it.

Withdrawing under the bedclothes again, Sybil closed her eyes and was once more almost dropping into unconsciousness when she heard the same series of noises: quite distinct now, deep in the house. The patter of small feet on the bare boards and a light noise which could have been a laugh.

In a second the fear passed, and she knew what it was. Marina still used the little room next to the nursery, but she was a sound sleeper, attending to the child before she went to bed and not waking again before her alarm roused her around seven. They always left the landing light burning through the night, and there was a small electric night light beside Helen's bed. Sybil smiled to herself: the child had obviously woken up and was now roaming the landing in search of mischief. She had done it already, once or twice, in London.

Not wishing to bother Joseph, who had a tendency

119

to be crusty if awakened at any time other than normal, she slid herself out of bed, groped for her housecoat and made her way gingerly through the darkness towards the door.

The landing was empty and silent, the boards rough to the bare soles of her feet; fleetingly she thought of splinters, hesitating, then rejecting the fuss of having to make her stealthy way back into the bedroom for her mules.

Helen was safe in bed, fast asleep, the bed unruffled, her hair in an untidy mass on the pillow. The child had not stirred since Marina last tucked her in. As she retraced her footsteps down the corridor to the landing, Sybil began to feel a tingle of fear, the nape of her neck prickling and a coldness spreading up her back. She had not been dreaming, on that last occasion. She had heard the noise of small feet and a childlike laugh. One of the boards moved, cold under her foot, and she stood at the stair-head listening for the slightest sound coming from within the depths of the silent house.

She tried to rationalise. An animal? she wondered. A squirrel, perhaps, trapped inside the empty skirting boards, or in the wide loft which ran under the eaves? Birds in one of the chimneys? Big old houses, she knew, had their own sounds, their particular groans: the fabric against the elements—like wooden sailing ships. Her neck tingled again and there was a sharp creaking sound from somewhere below. A small footstep? Or simply the woodwork? Joseph said they must expect some noise from the timbers as they dried out, giving up the damp accumulated while the place stood empty. The silence bore in on her again and she began to move towards the bedroom door.

A small animal? The woodwork? Her imagination? A dream? As she felt Joseph's body comfortingly close to her in the bed, so the fear started to recede. It was only then that she remembered Helen's chatter about the crying baby, the story of the tragedy and the rustle of wings outside the window.

She shivered, even in the warmth, and took a long while to find sleep again.

In the morning, as often happens with night-time disturbances, she was unable to make up her mind about the incident: even uncertain about standing on the landing and hearing the creaking below.

Marina brought in their tea as usual, Helen stumping along behind clutching the papers and mail, boisterous and full of the idea of Christmas—about which Marina had obviously been telling her. In the midst of all the noise (which was part of the morning game of "waking up Daddy"), Sybil was surprised to hear Marina telling her that she would be going up to the village for the sugar in a little while.

"You haven't been yet?" trying to work out how the girl had managed.

"No, I go in a minute. Not terribly important. No rush." She made a dive for Helen, who was in danger of rolling off the bed as she tormented her father.

"But was there enough for the tea—and for you?"
Perhaps Marina and Helen had not yet had breakfast.

"There's plenty (Helen, come on, stand up properly.
Poor Daddy). Plenty. A full bowl."

"But there was hardly any left last night."

"No." Marina laughed, thinking it was funny. "No,
the bowl full to the top. You must fill it last night."

"But there wasn't any . . ." Sybil stopped herself. "I
must be dotty," she said to Joseph later.

"I could've sworn the sugar bowl was nearly empty.
We had none in the house."

"Your mind was on other things last night, Angel.
Keeping your man happy." He reached down under the
covers to stroke her, his eyes shining with pleasure.
"Today," he announced, "I finish with the work early.
I telephone the office; deal with what has to be done,
then we go out and get the *tannenbaum*."

"Tannenbaum?" she laughed. "Did you call it a tannenbaum in Denmark? I thought that was a German
word. Christmas tree."

His expression changed, a slight frown, his eyes distant, as though trying to see over some far horizon.

"Oh yes. Christmas tree. You forget, Angel, when I
was a little boy there were many German soldiers
around. Yes, they called it a tannenbaum. They sang:
'Oh Tannenbaum; Oh Tannenbaum . . .'"

That afternoon they drove into Farnham and bought
baubles and glass balls, fairy lights that went on and

off, lametta, chocolate mice and Father Christmasses, and a beautiful silver star. They had not bought these things for the previous two Christmases. Helen had been too small last year to appreciate them. Now, at nearly two and a half, they thought she would enjoy the glitter.

On the way home they stopped at the Forestry Commission Centre and bought a tree—almost seven feet tall—then drove back to Tilt, setting the tree in a pot in the drawing room and, much to Helen's delight, decorating it so that it became a wondrous magical totem in the corner of the room. Even all this failed to drive away the nervousness which Sybil felt as night once more drew in around the house.

10

On the morning after the arrangement had been made
with Maitland-Wood, Tony Gibbs gave Cooling a Ministry pass. The porter made him sign in, and gave him
the keys.

"Room 421, sir. On the fourth floor," he said.

There was a double lock on the door; inside it was
furnished with a desk, two chairs, a telephone and a
table upon which the files were already stacked. He
realised that downstairs he had signed for the room
keys and the files.

As he was settling down, a girl arrived and said that
she had been assigned to him.

Her name was Heather and he judged her to be
about twenty: slim and dark, assured, with good legs.
With a few guarded questions, Cooling elicited that

she was not cleared to handle the files, only to run messages, type non-classified letters and memos, and get his tea. She gave him her office number and said that it was nice to have someone new in this part of the building. Then she left, with a smile which suggested that she would have dinner with him if he asked: and maybe more besides. Unusually sexist for her type of liberated woman, he thought.

He told himself to be careful. They were not above trying a bit of sanctification, if they wanted to draw him deeper into the clandestine side. Heather had that smart, plummy voice which spoke of a cut-glass background. The kind of girl the trade enjoyed using: the kind they called a lady.

Out of working hours, he had already decided, he would continue to read the historical background. In working hours he would trace through the files backwards, arriving finally at those bizarre last days in Berlin with as much current information as possible. When he reached that point, it would be like looking through the wrong end of a telescope anyway, so it might as well be a clean view.

He began with the latest crystal-gazer reports, which were all much as Maitland-Wood suggested: fear of economic collapse and the aftermath; fear of polarisation into two equally dangerous extreme groups, left and right; fear of the kind of demands these groups might make on any moderate government.

There was a list of variously graded undesirables on both sides of the fence: some clandestine. Werewolf was at the top of the list, and Cooling remembered the whole conception of what had been called Undertaking Werewolf, during the early stages of the final battle for Berlin: the Werewolves conceived as terrorist groups— men, women and children—to fight and harass behind Allied lines. For a time there had even been a Radio Werewolf, until Goebbels himself took it over to preach his odious dogma of total destruction. He wondered if Maitland-Wood's coding of the subject Werewolf had any subconscious connection with Undertaking Werewolf in 1945. It was not the first time that his mind had travelled into that particular tributary, in spite of his deeper feelings which branded the whole idea of Werewolf as nonsense.

Yet there were disturbing facts in Werewolf's personal file: the carefully planned establishing of residence; his naturalisation (spotted too late to be rescinded); the calculation of his marriage; most of all, the known contacts who had visited his office, or whom he had met during his travels in Europe: known fascist idealists, agitators, members of the Column 88, and other deeply secret neo-Nazi societies. His life before that, in Argentina and other Latin American countries, had brought him into continuous contact with fingered former SS and staunch Nazis; with the ludicrous Fourth Reich in Chile; with Bermann and Mengele, to name but two of the well-known orchestra.

Towards the end of his first day, Cooling was left frustrated. There were so many facts; and yet, even with this collated evidence, did they really take it seriously? Even as he sat here, a trial was taking place in Düsseldorf: sixteen men and women, ex-SS, on charges of atrocities and murder in the Polish concentration camp at Maidanek. Thirty years after, there was still a loathing. So, did they really believe that the English right wing would fall victim to the uncertain claimant of the subjugated and destroyed Reich Chancellery?

Yet, of course, the man was in deep cover, with a British passport and the rights of a British citizen. He was not a wanted war criminal. It occurred to Cooling that Maitland-Wood's talk of action might be overstepping his brief. This evaluation could simply be required to firm up the evidence. Not for action now, but for use in emergency; in case Werewolf did the unthinkable and tried for a place in British politics, still within his cover. Or, perhaps there was so much to be done, such an enormous bureaucratic backlog, that the department preferred to spend its time sorting through trivia; raising bogies where none existed.

Heather brought him coffee in the morning, tea in the afternoon, and lingered by the door, trying to chat with him. He was more convinced than ever that she was one of the ladies. He would have to get the job done as quickly as possible. Shut away in this silent room above Whitehall would not do him any good. People on the clandestine side always said the initial sense of loneliness was the worst; the period before you really got down inside your cover and lived it. The first days were the ones which made you vulnerable; when, if you were not careful, the neuroticisms incubated inside. That same sense of vulnerability bred from actions like living in the house near St. James's, spending the day in the one room working through the past with ghosts, aware of the shadows watching your back wherever you went.

It might well turn out that Maitland-Wood could require him to perform an operation which he may judge personally or morally unsound. It was a perfectly natural step, in the minds of people like the Deputy Director, to soften him up, create barriers between him and the world, offer him pieces of cake, like Heather: the sweetening. You did not have to be well versed in their methods to read the scenario. The friendship, the compromise, then the news. The news? Perhaps, after one day, he was getting paranoid: but maybe the news was already set to be laid on him. Heather was not cleared for the files. The files had been stacked here in the office when he arrived. There needed only to be one problem with classified material and he would be in a position of compromise.

So he showed Heather the door, and tried to remember all the things he knew from people familiar with the trade. He needed some kind of insurance, so he picked up the telephone and got through to the Deputy Director's office. The Deputy Director would not be back until after Christmas, a drawling lady told him.

He dialled the main desk downstairs.

"I signed in this morning for the keys of Room 421. Cooling," he said. "I also signed for a batch of files already assembled in this room. Would you send the duplicate sheet up here straight away."

The porter tried to argue, so he told the man that he was working under the instructions of the Deputy Director. The duplicate sheet was on his desk within three minutes. Stapled to it was the list of files, countersigned by Head of Registry. Against his own signature was his time of arrival. It took twenty minutes to check off the files. They were all present, so he rang the Duty Officer.

When he arrived, the Duty Officer looked tired and harassed; a thin young man with a certain agility of movement and hard eyes. His name was Finnemore and he was inclined to be unfriendly.

"What's the trouble?"

Cooling told him that he wanted security on the files out to him from Registry. "I don't want to be caught short. In future I shall require the DO's countersignature when I arrive and before I leave."

Finnemore cast an eye over the stack of files, noted the number of red bindings, then went over to the tele-

phone, picking it up as though performing a silent kill.
For five minutes he lectured Head of Registry on the
dangers of files being out on permanent call to one
office: particularly classified material.

Five minutes later a dubious clerk arrived, checked
the files against her list, countersigned and wheeled
them away.

"I don't want any of that stuff delivered to this office
until I call through for it each morning," Cooling told
him, feeling pleased with himself.

"Shade slipshod," Finnemore said as he left. "Just
to save themselves five minutes night and morning.
Anything had gone wrong, you'd have been in it up to
your ears. I don't understand them."

Cooling did not tell him that he understood them
only too well. When he got downstairs, Heather was
signing out.

"I give you a lift, Mr. Cooling?" She had a fresh coat
of war paint and was all breathless. "Got the car just
around the corner." Her tongue darting between her
lips.

"I'm walking," he said, grinning, "but thanks for the
offer."

"Any time."

The shadows were still with him all the way back,
though they could not get close when he used the telephone box in the Trafalgar Square post office.

He called Steph's office. Yes, she was back from New
York, but had gone home. Did he know her home num-

ber? He did, and dialled it. After fifteen rings he gave up.

"Hear you've been making a fuss about the files," Gibbs said over dinner, his voice lofty, as though Cooling had been engaging in some pettiness which should really have been above him.

"I should bloody well think so. I'm not carrying cans for anyone."

"Yes. Can't think what got into them. The DD's orders were plain enough."

"I bet they were." He speared a piece of meat angrily. "While you're at it, Tony, take the lady off my back. If I want a girl, I'll find a clean one."

Gibbs looked shocked, like a prissy academic hearing that his best piece of work had been blown. "I'm sure I don't know what you mean."

"I've no intention of lying in the heather. So call her off."

After dinner he went out again and rang Steph's number from the call box on the corner. There was still no reply and he was nervous for the rest of the evening.

II

They had moved Heather by the second day, replacing her with a plump, brisk, efficient girl called Mary, whom Cooling decided was no lady in the technical sense. He worked on, backwards through the files, tracing Werewolf's career in reverse, like a time machine.

By mid-morning he became conscious of anxiety spreading from the fact that he had not yet been able to get hold of Steph. It was like a vicious circle, the anxiety followed by the questioning of his conscience. Why was he so concerned? She did not know he was in London. There was no great plot to keep them apart. In the end he decided that jealousy was involved; for he had asked himself, a number of times, about where she was likely to have been on the previous evening; and who could she have been with? It was a manifestation of the truth: he had missed her more than he would admit.

Around eleven-thirty, Cooling double-locked his room and signed out of the building, conscious that the files were still stacked on the table, which meant he was taking a minute security risk.

A hundred yards up the road he knew the shadows were not there. They were trusting him as a person of routine; a man of habit as far as work was concerned. It was a point worth remembering.

She was in her office and they put him through straight away. He noticed the odd butterfly feeling in his stomach, a dryness in the throat, and a sense of being flattered when she was so plainly surprised and delighted to hear his voice.

"It couldn't be more wonderful," she said. "You're the one person in the world I'd really like to see at this moment."

Those kinds of superlatives were unusual for Steph. Cooling's mind split in two: the professional in him whispering caution; the man elated. Somehow he had expected that it would all be an anti-climax. Instead he found it exciting. They arranged dinner at Chez Solange for that evening, and he rang Gibbs when he got back into the office to say that he would not be in to dinner.

"Found a clean girl, have you?" Gibbs sounded quite nasty.

"An old friend."

Cooling knew they would have the details anyway: if not at that precise moment, at least by tomorrow. To hell with that. She was an old friend of the Hardwickes, and they would have nudged him about her before now if there had been any sensitive problems.

An hour later, while he was working his way through the labyrinths of intrigue which Werewolf had used to establish his Danish cover (or to be correct, which others had used to help him), Gibbs appeared in person, clutching a red file as though he had given birth.

"The first wire transcriptions," he said cryptically. "You'll be getting them once every two days. Back to me, tonight at the house if you please. The Deputy Director says they're to be kept there."

"I'd like to sign for them just the same." Taking no chances. He would be jumping at his own shadow next.

A lot of it was domestic stuff, Werewolf's wife fixing up a dental appointment, a Mrs. Mountford ringing to welcome them to the village and asking if they could come to a small cocktail party on Boxing Day. She accepted, Cooling called his mother on the office phone and asked her if there was any chance of being invited.

"I saw Mrs. Mountford this morning, dear. She's an old bridge chum. She and the Colonel play regularly."

Yes, she had been invited and they had asked her to bring her son along.

Maitland-Wood should be pleased when he heard that—as he doubtlessly would by tomorrow.

Most of the remaining wire transcriptions were between Werewolf and the queen bee at his office. Lots of stuff about orders, letters, cash flow, movement of furniture into the country. It would be as well to have these checked by the import people, but it sounded genuine enough. There were two incoming calls from unidentified males (*Note from wireman: No time or sophistication, as yet, to check origin of calls*) who appeared to be part-time representatives of Werewolf's firm. On both occasions the possibility of a conference early in spring was mentioned. Another incoming call was from a woman. It made little sense.

> Werewolf: Hallo.
>
> Caller: I had a message.
>
> W: Oh, it's you. Yes, I just wanted to make certain that you were keeping an eye on things.
>
> C: I've told you already, I don't know anyone in this country. It was different on the Continent, but here I'm a nobody.
>
> W: Never say that, my dear. Don't forget, you were recommended to me especially.
>
> C: On the Continent, fine, but here I'm out of play.
>
> W: Okay. I'm not expecting problems, but if you do make any contacts, we're always interested.
>
> C: I won't forget.
>
> W: I'm sure you won't.

Cooling sniffed. It sounded like trade jargon—his kind of trade jargon, though you could never tell. It did, however, breathe a little speculation, a shade of intrigue, among the other, seemingly dull telephone chat. A few more like that and he would actually start believing in Werewolf's potential danger.

There was another call which left Cooling uneasy. This time it was a man.

Werewolf: Gotterson.

Caller: Ah, Mr. Gotterson, I've found you at last. It's Rivers. Michael Rivers.

W: Yes?

C: We spoke. Last year in Sweden. Remember?

W: Yes, I remember.

C: I thought we should talk again.

W: We have nothing to talk about at the moment.

C: You could be very useful to us, Mr. Gotterson. When the time comes you could be very useful. Your advice and knowledge. After all, a man with your background . . .

W: Forget about my background. That has nothing to do with it. You don't know anything about my background.

C: The past always has a bearing on the present.

W: I'm not prepared . . .

C: Your personal history would interest a lot of people.

W: What possible interest . . . ?

C: When can we meet?

W: Not for some time.

C: Don't throw away the chance to serve, Mr. Gotterson. After all, tradition is . . .

W: Go to hell.

The name Michael Rivers rang some kind of bell but Cooling could not quite put his finger on the button. That evening he took a cab back to the house with the wire transcriptions in his briefcase. Gibbs signed for them.

"Rivers?" Cooling asked.

"That's got everyone worried. There's just been the one call and our people hadn't even logged the fact of their meeting last year in Sweden."

"No." Cooling shook his head. "Who is he?"

"Michael Rivers? Political dabbler. If he was a Marxist we'd probably say activist instead of dabbler. Anti-Communist; secretary of the British League."

"Far right as that?" He raised his eyebrows.

"So far right he almost meets himself on the way back. Stood twice as an independent; supporter of private armies; keep Britain white, all that kind of thing . . ."

"Got him." Cooling remembered now. "He wrote a book."

Gibbs nodded, *Towards A National Britain.*

So that was the bone upon which the crystal-gazers, the Minister and Maitland-Wood gnawed. A small bone, but a bone nevertheless. He told Gibbs that he would be late back, and for his pains received an acid remark about burning the candle at both ends.

Steph was waiting for him when he arrived at Chez Solange. He had booked a table in the small upstairs room, and she was waiting for him in the bar. As he came to the top of the stairs he saw her, sitting alone, one hand playing with the stem of her glass, her face grave and pensive, as if there was something worrying her. She looked as neat as ever, but a shade thinner.

There was no doubt that she was pleased to see him. Like her enthusiastic remarks on the telephone, her greeting was far more effusive than he ever remembered from Berlin. In fact he was slightly concerned, for she seemed to cling to him for a moment.

No, she had not liked New York, it had been bloody hard work, but then it was all bloody hard work and she did not care for London any more. How was Berlin? How long was he here for? "And what are you doing here?" Her hand went to her mouth, "Oh, I'm sorry, Vincent. I know I'm not allowed to ask. I'm sorry."

He shook his head. "I'm on a course. Nothing dreadful."

She changed the subject and for a while they talked, enthusiastically, about Berlin. "It seems so long ago now." She was almost wistful. Had he seen any new films? She had thought some movie, by a director he had never heard of, was wonderful. There appeared to be a dearth of good novels, but had he read the latest Deighton, and what did he think of it? What was he doing for Christmas? Yes, she was going home as well: Norfolk, the first time she had been at home with her parents for ages. No, she wasn't really looking forward to it.

"It is wonderful to see you again, love. Truly." She put her hand out over the table to touch him. "Nothing's been the same since Berlin." Again that sudden grave look in her eyes.

"Nothing wrong, is there?"

"Of course not. I'm just a mite tired. The job could be going better," a little smirk, "and really I am a bit disenchanted with London. It's all such a sweat."

He knew instinctively that she was going to ask if they could go to bed. "I can't take you home, I'm afraid," he told her, amazed that his voice cracked slightly. "It's like living in the YMCA."

She laughed and looked very happy for a moment. "No need. You come to my place." She lowered her voice and narrowed her eyes, in a jokey *femme fatale* impression. "I'm all on my lonesome and I've got a big double bed."

She must have seen the look cross his face: he felt his mouth move involuntarily.

"No, Vincent, there's nobody else at the moment." She smiled, pleased with her mind-reading.

He could hardly believe he was telling her that he loved her, but it came out, like something rushing from the subconscious under one of the interrogation drugs: the kind that make you very articulate. But he told her as they made love, and again after it was over in the splendid bedroom of her little flat near Cheyne Walk.

"We have got something a bit special, haven't we, Vincent?" Looking up at him, hard, the worried expression still there. It was as though she was asking for some kind of reassurance, and as if it mattered greatly.

"I think so. Do you want . . . ?"

"Marriage? I don't know. It was marriage you were going to say, wasn't it?"

It was; and that, again, surprised him.

"What about you?" she asked.

He did not know either.

"Let's leave it as it is for the time being." She turned away. "Vincent, I've got a couple of problems at the moment. I can't really think straight. I'll have it cleared up by the time Christmas is over. Bear with me."

"Another fellow?" He felt confused, both by his own reactions to their reunion, and by her attitude: the effusiveness, the obvious need, the troubled look.

"Not really. No. I'll tell you all about it when it's over. There's nothing to worry about." Her hand reached up, a finger traced down the side of his cheek, then dropped to his thighs and they began again.

"I've missed you such a lot," she said as he was getting ready to leave. "At first I thought it was just Berlin, then I realised it was you. I didn't know how to tell you in a letter."

"I know. I know exactly what you mean."

He remembered their parting in Berlin—"No sad goodbyes. It's not like that, is it?" she had said—and was now almost amazed at the change in her. It was as though they were both on the edge of some precipice and in desperate need of each other's assistance. It was not simply the physical requirement of their bodies, but somehow a great boosting high at being in each other's company. No, it was more than that, and it had him confused, as though he was in a maze of mirrors.

They arranged to meet on the following night. She would cook for him, she said, and how did he fancy boiled cornflakes? She had once told him that when she was a youngster her mother had despaired of her ever being able to cook—"You're the kind of girl who'd fry an egg with the shell on and boil cornflakes." It was a family joke.

There were no taxis, so Cooling started to walk. Five paces and the warning sounded in his head. He saw one of the shadows detach itself from the darkness, and in that second, Cooling could have sworn that another figure was left there, watching the house in which Steph had her flat.

Gibbs waived the silent breakfast rule the next morning, sending the slaves packing as soon as Cooling appeared.

"This came in late last night. I've talked to the DD and he says you should read it before you go in." It was a wire transcription again. "The last one," Gibbs told him, pointing to the final page.

Werewolf was talking to the queen bee at his office.

QB: And you're settling down, are you?
W: Yes, yes, very nicely really. I think you'll like the place when we've got it organised.
QB: I'm longing to see it.

(They spoke in English though her accent was more marked than his, said a note at the start of the sequence.)

W: The only thing . . .
QB: Yes?
W: Well, to be honest, my wife's having a bit of trouble. There's a story about the house. We came across it almost by accident. A nasty story about a child being killed here. Killed by a bird.
QB: Oh, gracious. She's nervous for little Helen.
W: Nervous. Yes. A little frightened. I think she's susceptible to atmosphere. I hadn't realised. She says she's heard things. In the night. The child also, Helen. The maid's nervous as well—superstitious girl. It doesn't worry me, and I think only my wife sometimes.
QB: She believes in ghosts?

W: She says not, but there is no doubt the house is noisy. Like a lot of old houses. She says she would not like to be here on her own. I try to make light of it, but it makes me nervous. I am most concerned for her, and for little Helen. It is not pleasant, you know, to see them so anxious. They are frightened—bad dreams and that kind of thing.

QB: Perhaps when the summer comes it will get better: when she becomes more used to the house.

W: We hope so. It worries me greatly.

QB: Oh, I'm sure she'll get used to it. We're living in 1975 now. You must tell her that. Try to make her see it in the right proportion. Now, I have had a telephone call from Manchester, from the store . . .

"Things that go bump in the night," Cooling said, smiling.

"The Deputy Director suggests that you look into it over Christmas. He understands that you've already made arrangements to make contact."

"Oh, you never close, do you? I thought you'd like that one. I did it especially to show my undying loyalty to Reichführer Maitland-Wood."

"We are wired here as well." Gibbs looked down his nose.

"It wouldn't be home if you weren't." He thought of

the previous night. "You're not involving my friends in any of this, are you, Tony?"

"Why should we?"

"Well, don't. I wouldn't like that at all. My mother's different, she's family. But not anyone else."

"It is my experience." Gibbs put on his pompous voice: the university don. "It's my experience that people tend to get themselves involved with us rather than the other way around."

"Yes." He knew the sinister, black side as well as anyone. "It's the difference between pure and applied research, isn't it?"

"Something like that. Why go looking for people when they come to you in the end with their balls on a silver platter?"

"Thank God I only evaluate. The trade has no morals."

"That's not quite true, Vincent. The trade looks at morals from a different standpoint, that's all. There's another thing."

"Rivers again?"

"No. The Deputy Director has a whisper from one of our people in publishing."

Cooling waited.

"You've heard of Robin Chilton?"

"Wrote a book about Bormann?"

"That's the one. Claimed he'd met him."

"I've read it."

"He's just submitted a new manuscript. In draft at

the moment, but a cause for concern. It's called *The Next Reich*."

"No prizes. The South American Nazis? Right?"

"There are several pages on Max Kritter—Moonlight. Nobody has ever written about him before."

"And?"

"And it's only a draft. He's doing some more work on the man he calls Kritter's son. The boy companion in exile. He could stumble over the truth."

"Then it gets blown, doesn't it?" Cooling felt a small upward surge of elation. It would be the best thing. Let someone else blow it sky high; reveal it for what it was—a dream game; an obsessional, neurotic game for men like Maitland-Wood; a method of passing the years in the autumn of their professional lives.

In the days before Christmas, Sybil was too busy to surrender to her nervousness during the light hours. Helen, with no idea of what Christmas was all about, knew only that it was special; listening wide-eyed and with increasing wild excitement to the sentimentalities of the baby Jesus' story, as told to her by Marina, and with awesome expectancy to the whole fabrication of Christmas stockings, presents under the tree and the barely understood rituals which already marked the season as a magic time.

It was only when night came and the restless child was settled that Sybil's imagination ran riot. Each creak and footfall became a matter for questioning, and twice in the small hours she was wakened by what, in the end, she decided were projections of her own nervousness.

Helen mentioned the baby again on the day before Christmas Eve. "The baby waked me up last night, Mummy. Is it the baby Jesus?"

The placid Marina was also nervous and declared the house to be "noisy at night."

Joseph remained calm, joking and poo-pooing the restlessness of the place, telling her that imagination had got the better of her.

Yet this was only his own self-discipline. Inside, his concern was acute. As a husband and father it was difficult to remain unmoved by the strange fancies which seemed to infest his loved ones.

On Christmas Eve, Sybil hung a holly wreath on the front door and, hearing a noise which she took to be the postman, late in the afternoon, discovered the wreath on the floor of the porch. It was also on Christmas Eve that the kitchen scissors were lost. One minute she was using them to cut the stems from a pile of wild Christmas roses she had gathered from their jungle garden; the next they were gone. Joseph was in the study and Marina had taken the child for a long walk around the village in a futile attempt to tire her before nightfall.

When she went to see Helen in bed and supervise the hanging up of the little white stocking, Sybil discovered the scissors under the cot, and, when she went to the main bedroom to draw the curtains, again thought she could hear the rustle of wings in the trees outside the window.

The experiences did not produce in her any sense of fear or terror. She was a rational woman, yet could not deny an anxiety and nervousness: a hollow feeling that the house contained some activity beyond its inhabitants, as though it was the vortex of desperate memories.

In London, Cooling saw Steph three more times before Christmas Eve. They remained on neutral ground, talking much of the days of their first relationship in Berlin, hardly touching on the present, making no specific plans for the future, as though they were both loath to commit themselves.

But they were more than comfortable in each other's company, the ease they felt only slightly jarred by Steph's occasional lapses into silence. Her problems, he decided, were preying on her mind, but she assured him that nothing drastic was going on. It would all be cleared up once the holiday was past.

The shopping crowds and the whole commercial rush of the season flowed past them, for they had no personal preparations to make—above buying small gifts for each other (cuff-links for Cooling, an extravagant box of toiletries for Steph) and presents for their respective families—easier for Cooling, for he had only his mother to think of.

They ate mainly in Steph's flat, lazing away the evenings and making love with a confidence which had no time for any distractions.

During the days, Cooling worked on through the files. By the evening of the twenty-third, he found that the journey had taken him back, almost to the last days in Berlin. The conclusions were clear and inescapable. SS Sturmbannführer Kritter (Moonlight) had left Berlin around May 1, 1945, with a young boy (Werewolf). They had made their way to Spain and from there to Latin America. In the years that followed, Kritter had treated the boy like a son. Money was available, connections with former Nazis were clear and made stronger as time progressed. Werewolf had established a Danish citizenship and then became a naturalised British citizen in circumstances which could only be classed as clandestine. After Kritter's death he had married an English girl, and for some time now the couple had lived in England. They had one child.

As to Werewolf's identity, real or presumed, this was a different matter, and Cooling was not prepared to start an examination of the facts—meagre as they were —until after the holiday was over.

On Christmas Eve he went into the office and wrote a long private memo to the Deputy Director, with a copy to Gibbs, in which he asked for certain items to be made available during the following week. Among these he included all film and photographs, known and authenticated, taken in or near the Reich Chancellery bunkers during the last few days of the Third Reich. In particular he wanted to view, at length, the film of Hitler investing members of the Hitler Youth with the Iron Cross on his birthday—April 20, 1945—together with all published Russian photographs of the corpses found in and around the bunkers.

At midday, the rest of the building was bubbling and in festive mood. Like any other office party. It took over half an hour to get the files returned to Registry, and when it was finally done Cooling returned to the house, packed his bag and took a train from Waterloo to Farnham. From there, after a long wait, he secured a taxi to Tilt, where his mother awaited him, a small Christmas tree in her living-room window, sprigs of holly over the pictures, unopened bottles on the sideboard, and a delicious smell of baking coming from her kitchen. It reminded Cooling so much of his childhood that he experienced a rare sense of emotional nostalgia followed by deep gloom, centered around both his task and this small separation from Steph.

The task occupied many of his waking thoughts, for he was conscious that the ciphers which were Werewolf would soon appear before him in flesh and blood. God knew where that might lead him.

Book Two:

SPECTRES OF THE PRESENT

12

There is nothing Old World, charming, or chocolate box about the village of Tilt. No tourists flock there in summer to admire thatched cottages, eat cream teas in inglenooks, or touch antiquity within the prosaic little church. For Tilt is an ugly, and relatively modern, village.

There is evidence that a small settlement existed on the site of the present village at the time of the Doomsday Book, and its name is thought by reputable local historians to be derived from the Anglo-Saxon word *teld*—meaning tent. But no trace of Saxon ancestry remains, and the oldest standing building, Tilt Hall, dates indisputably from 1832.

The Hall, the creation of a demonic beer baron, is Gothic and ghastly, shuffling several architectural styles into one huge lump of spires, turrets and castellations. It has only two small claims to fame: the great W. G. Grace once played cricket on the huge lawn, and the progressive school—which took over the building in the late 1920s—received some sensational publicity from the national press during the early 1970s over the question of drugs, drink and illicit sex.

Tilt Hall lies, bedded in spacious grounds, at the southern extremity of the village, high on rising ground so that from its ornate terraces, and lower garden walks, there are beautiful sweeping views across the green and gold chequerboard of Hampshire.

The Hall is linked to the small huddle of Victorian buildings which make up the focal point of the village, by a straight beech-lined road—known as the Main Road (which it is not). This avenue, running for approximately half a mile, has over the years acquired more than beech trees. A spate of property development in the early 1930s brought to its boundaries a series of select detached dwelling houses, each with a brutal charm of its own.

They stand back from the road, mock Tudor vying with sunburst stained glass, their names displayed on hanging wrought-iron frames or carved and polished sections of tree trunk: *Silver Birches* (where no birches appear to grow); *Twin Elms* (gone with the Dutch disease); *Willows* (which are not visible). This is the Nobs' Hill of the community: commuter land, from whence smooth executives set out daily to bustle in the city, or can be seen on Sundays cleaning the shining Audi or Jaguar, bush-puppied, plump in cable-stitched sweaters, before riding over to the nearest smart pub—somewhere near Frensham Ponds—for the lunchtime jar.

Just before the Main Road reaches the cluster of the village centre, it is broken, on one side, by the village hall (circa 1932), on the other by a slip road which is flanked by smaller though equally select houses. This is the High Street, though there is not one shop in sight, known to waggish locals as the Brigadier Belt, for here there lives a high concentration of retired service officers and their wives, struggling on pensions against the final tide.

The Main Road expands as it reaches the village proper: a widening into a small ellipse around which a few shops compete, and the pub, The Crossways (light lunches, snacks, no coaches), stands in pink solitude. The buildings are plainly Victorian: the Post Office Stores, directly opposite the pub, and a ragged straggle of butcher, news agent and grocer, their modernised façades garishly at variance with the depressing dullness of the buildings.

The Main Road continues on, forming one side of the triangle which makes up the recreation ground, the second side of which runs left, at an angle, past the Post Office Stores with its rusting metal advertisement for *Camp Coffee*, and gold-printed free-standing letters, *Hovis*, above the name board.

This is Cricket Lane, an alley which cuts between the five or six acres of common ground and a low volley of bungalows desperately fighting for individuality with names like *Boundary View, Recreation Cottage* and *Sydwin.*

In turn, Cricket Lane empties onto another, smaller ellipse in the centre of which stands the war memorial, with its bleak list of names, repeated, it seems, tragically, in two wars. To the left, Church Lane traces a winding path to, not unnaturally, the church; St. Peter's, small and pompous, built at the same time as the Hall. To the right, Scholars Road makes up the third side of the recreation ground. More bungalows, and in their midst the grey little village school poking its tiny open bell tower above the low roofs.

At the far end of Scholars Road, a little before it completes the link with the Main Road, stand two much larger houses. On the left, behind high walls, a line of tall Wellingtonias and a driveway encroached upon by spreading rhododendrons, is the red-brick cruciform of Pine Copse End. Across the road, a little nearer to the junction with the Main Road, stands the larger, more octagonal Heath Corner, known for many years now as The Flats.

Once the proud, uneconomic residence of a Farnham doctor, Heath Corner was neatly converted into seven modern and self-contained flats in the years immediately following the second world war, and it now houses two widowers, three widows (one sharing with her sister) and a pair of retired couples. The top floor flat nearest the road was, at this time, occupied by Mrs. Brenda Cooling.

On Christmas morning, the bells rang out from St. Peter's, the faithful drove and walked to worship, while the rest of the village secured themselves behind closed doors, preparing for the more gluttonous pagan ceremonies of the festival. Some gathered in The Crossways and a few, mainly children, braced themselves for gastronomic feats by a brisk walk around the recreation ground.

Some watched.

Cooling, standing a little back from his mother's living-room window, trained his binoculars through the swaying Wellingtonias onto the leaded windows of Pine Copse End.

"I think I shall indulge in a little sherry." Mrs. Cooling, coming from her bedroom, stood behind her son. "You fancy a spot?"

In her late sixties, she was still an immensely handsome woman; spry, clear-eyed, she had made her way through life, brought up her son without the help of a husband, and emerged, as a dauntless personality, having spent her working life in the harsh world of property development. Now, retirement had brought its just rewards, some of which glittered around the fingers of her right hand as it patted the upswept blue-rinsed hair.

The Christmas smells still percolated from the kitchen, and Cooling, adjusting his binoculars, murmured that he would prefer a gin and tonic to sherry.

"What's so interesting, dear?" She touched his shoulder and strode heavily to the sideboard.

"Nice house." Cooling turned back into the room and subsided into an armchair, waiting for the drink with pleasant anticipation.

"New people there." His mother reached over with the glass, taking her own to the other chair. "Gotterson, they're called. Mr. and Mrs. Gotterson." She lit a king-sized filter, peeling it from her lips and glancing at the resultant lipstick trace with a look of mild disgust.

"You met them yet?"

"Seen them. Not met them. They've a nice little girl as well. Seen her, too, and heard her, in the village. Father, mother, little girl and maid. You interested, dear?"

"Could be."

She raised her eyebrows, sipping at her sherry as though it was medicine. "Not clients, are they?"

There is a fiction which exists only outside the trade that once you are in the business of security your life remains secret except to your colleagues. It is nonsense, of course. Close relatives always know, though they rarely pry.

"I think they might possibly be clients." Cooling's voice reflected the fatigue he felt concerning the whole matter. He looked up quickly at his mother, the glance taking in any minute change in her expression: any hint of reaction.

"Oh dear," she murmured. "They seem so nice. Vincent, I didn't think you worked . . ." She stopped short, reining in on natural curiosity.

"I don't." Snapped like the loading mechanism of an automatic pistol. "This is something different. Special. I hope that you won't be bothered."

"Which means I might be."

Cooling cursed to himself. This was not what he wanted. He'd had enough of Werewolf's spectre grinning at him from the pages of files. What he really wanted—needed—was Christmas with Steph. A warm hotel, perhaps, where everything was laid on, and you could relax without having to look over your shoulder, without jumping at your shadow. More to the point, he wanted to exercise the ghosts of the officer and the boy stumbling over the rubble to the *danse macabre* of gunfire.

There was no peace or good will here, even snug by his own mother's hearth, for Werewolf brooded over the village, across the road in Pine Copse End, like a long and sinister shadow falling across one's door.

He stood up, leaned against the chair and looked out over the recreation ground, where more families were now trudging around, getting steam up for the turkey and pudding. The view stretched right over to the Post Office Stores, and down by the tripartite junction of Cricket Lane, Church Lane and Scholars Road he could see people coming past the war memorial and

cars dispersing. Morning service was over and the good
Christians were going, cleansed, to their homes to sin
no more.

"Can I help?" She took his glass gently from his
hand, moving over to refill it.

"You've probably helped already."

"Oh?"

"The party, tomorrow."

"Party? Oh, the Mountfords. I think you'll find that
rather a bore. It's not a party, just drinks before lunch.
The usual airing of snobbery. Showing off the new
clothes and bits of jewellery. They're an awful cliquey
lot, you know."

"They'll be looking at their new residents as well."

"Who? The Gottersons? You know that for sure?"

"They've been invited and they've accepted."

She came to stand beside him, leaving a fresh drink
in his hand. He wondered if Gibbs and Maitland-Wood
had the shadows still on him, and where the wireman
was hiding.

"You're very well informed," said his mother. There
was perhaps a hint of concern in her voice.

"Just pretend you didn't hear that. Behave normally." He sighed, knowing that she could keep up a
front but would still be worried. "That house? Pine
Copse End? Anything odd about it?"

"It's been empty a while. They've only just moved
in, but you would know that, wouldn't you? Yes, there
are odd tales. Every village has to have its haunted
house. Villages like their fantasies. There has to be a

village charmer, that's Mr. Dowdswell, no end of a lad
with the ladies; there has to be a village tart, we've got
at least two; then there's the village mystery, old Miss
Brackenridge at (would you believe?) *Holly Cottage.*"
She took a deep breath. "There has to be a village
adultery—I know of four possibles, though the people I
play bridge with are certain of six. The village idiot,
poor little Jeremy. The village gossip—full house. We
have all the standard requirements, so there has to be a
haunted house, and that's Pine Copse End."

She told him the story of Miss Ayerton and the child.
"Nearly everyone remembers her, and everybody
knows the story. The real villagers remember it, of
course. They say that in the last few years she talked of
it a great deal. There's a tradition that she was a recluse: another fantasy, because she played whist regularly—at home, not in the village hall—and she did not
play bridge. She had people in to little supper parties
until a couple of years before she died. But she talked
about it a lot, and that helped the legend. She used to
speak as if the child was still there: used to say that he
was a little devil, a mischief-maker, hid things and
played tricks on her. A bit loopy in the last few years."

"And the stories persist?"

"Of course they do. Not just persist: they're fos-
tered."

"And what do the locals say about the Gottersons?"

"They say he's well heeled; in furniture; a bit foreign." As though you could be a bit dead or a bit pregnant.

Cooling smiled, raising his glass to her. "Here's to the damnation of all those who are a bit foreign, eh, Mother?"

She gave a little laugh. Then—"Is there going to be unpleasantness?" The stolid middle-class fear asserting itself.

"I shouldn't think so for a minute."

Silently he thought of the great British understatement: the little bit of unpleasantness between 1939 and 1945: and those who suggested that a descendant of the heart of that unpleasantness was living just across the road.

"And if there was, you wouldn't tell me, and quite right as well."

"There's nothing to tell, Mum. Nothing," he lied.

In the silence which followed, Cooling looked around the room with its sensible furniture, the reproduction pictures, the pieces of ritual holly and a mantelpiece parading Christmas cards. He breathed in the smell of cooking turkey and knew that, while he adored his mother, he would rather be anywhere but here: preferably with Steph, in spite of her terrible cooking.

He felt the chill go through him as his mother spoke again, her voice dropping to a whisper as though she could be overheard.

"If you look across the road now, you'll see them. All of them. They're coming out of the drive. And they've got a dog. That's a new acquisition."

The dog's name was Brownie: an Alsatian puppy (though Joseph insisted on calling him a German shepherd, which was, after all, more correct). While it was supposed to be Joseph's present to himself, the animal was an obvious delight to little Helen, who adored him instantly.

Sybil was uncertain. "Aren't they difficult with children, Alsatians?"

Joseph told her that they were perfectly safe if brought up with a child, or children, and as long as they did not get confused. There had to be one master only.

"I just thought I'd read about children being savaged . . ."

"It happens, but usually among people who don't know about dogs. I have been with dogs all my life, until we moved to Europe. There will be no danger."

They took him out on Christmas morning, after the opening of presents under the tree, more to walk off Helen's excitement than to exercise the dog.

It was an explosive morning which had begun at five o'clock, when Helen discovered her stocking full and brimming with interesting things which she insisted on showing to everybody. Sybil had almost forgotten the delicious feeling of secrets and surprises which invades a household with a young child: the tearing and scrabbling at the wrapping and the cries of delight. As Helen was overjoyed at the influx of good things—a Teddy bear, simple games, things to blow and hit, and

an amazing plastic train which played nursery tunes—
so the joy was reflected in Sybil as she opened her
gifts: a new pair of expensive boots (for which she had
asked), scent, the usual gift-wrapped unguents, a feast
of extravagant personal fripperies, and several books
she had long wanted yet could not recall mentioning.

For Joseph, the whole of Wagner's Ring Cycle in a
boxed set of LPs, a walking stick ("For getting around
the estate," laughed Sybil), male toiletries and a splendid smoking jacket.

They walked Brownie, who was docile, played with
Helen, ate huge portions of turkey, wore paper hats
and then, as night came down, gave Brownie his evening run, bathed the tearfully tired Helen and flopped
in front of the television.

Sybil woke once during the night and thought she
could hear the dog whining, but the day had so ex-
hausted her that she quickly dropped into sleep once
more.

So Christmas Day passed at Pine Copse End, and on
Boxing morning they were due for drinks at the
Mountfords'.

At a little after eleven on Boxing morning, the telephone rang in Mrs. Cooling's flat. Cooling, who was
preparing for the Mountfords' party, was surprised to
hear his mother call him.

It was Steph back in London, speaking from a call
box, distraught, tearful and needing to see him ur-
gently.

13

By design they arrived late at the Mountfords'. The little pebble-dashed house in the High Street appeared crushed and crowded with people: the swarming bee-like noise of thirty or forty voices seeping out over the small lawn, audible along the road, which was almost blocked by the lines of parked cars attesting to the fact of the Colonel's drinks party.

Steph was to drive down and would meet Cooling about two o'clock. She did not want to see, or meet, anyone else: she had been adamant about it, and nothing he could say on the crackling telephone line would budge her. In the end, he agreed, gladly, to drive back to London with her and could sense the relief in her voice, as though something terrible, trapped within her, had been released.

His mother asked no questions, accepting the change

of plan with quiet resignation, showing no outward sign of disappointment. She would get quietly drunk at the Mountfords', she claimed, and spend the rest of the day sleeping it off. Tomorrow there would be other things to do.

That Colonel Mountford had served in all parts of the globe was obvious. Mementos of his military life crowded the small white living room, jostling each other from mantelpiece and table, while in the hall regimental pictures hung to attention around a signed photograph of the great soldier of World War Two (*Proud to have served with you. Montgomery*).

Mrs. Mountford was a plump rubber-ball woman with a small voice which made her almost a caricature figure; and while she constantly referred to her husband as Benji, she managed to give the impression that she really wanted to speak of him only as the Colonel. In some ways she seemed to have pulled off a mental conjuring trick which made her immune to all forms of life except those with a service background, and Cooling's immediate feeling upon entering the house was one of being in the Officers' Mess on ladies' morning.

The Colonel himself was tall and thin, grey-haired, aquiline, crisp in both manner and voice. A bloody martinet, Cooling decided: a good colleague for Maitland-Wood.

Greeted in the hall, a huge gin and tonic pressed into his hand, Cooling was launched into the babble without benefit of either instructions or guidance. One had to fend for oneself, and his mother was carried away by the Colonel's lady into some side room where her bridge cronies chattered of Culbertson, double jumps, grand slams and presumably the six village adulteries.

He hesitated just inside the door of the crowded main room, noticing that in spite of the animated noise everyone was standing and behaving in a formal, almost too correct, manner.

For a moment he remained smiling on the fringe of four people who ignored him. A woman with an atrociously loud voice was telling a shy young man of her success in growing *courgettes* during the summer, while close by, a haughty red-haired lady with brittle eyes was talking to a smug-looking sleek man about the perils of teen-age children.

"I make it a rule," she drawled, "never to let them use the drawing room. After all, one keeps one's best things there. I forbid it completely. Let them have their heads, but some things are barred."

He pressed forward, gently looking for his quarry. To his right, a plump, balding Romeo confided that he had "gone after the daughter and ended up with the mother."

In the centre of the room he came up abruptly in front of a pair of middle-aged men, both sporting beards. They stopped talking as he faced them, eyeing him with shifty mistrust.

"Cooling," he said, trying to smile with a studied insouciance. "My mother lives in the village."

"Brent," the larger of the pair fixed him with watery eyes.

"Caswell," announced the other, then, almost with condescension, "You don't live here, then?"

"No. In Town. I live in London. Just here for Christmas."

"Fairly central?" from Brent.

"What line?" asked Caswell.

Cooling, uncertain whether he was enquiring about the nearest underground station or his work, plumped for the latter. "Research," he replied, staying in cover.

"Chemical?" pushed Brent.

"Industrial. Among other things."

"Difficult time for you fellows, then." Brent appeared quite disinterested. "Ah, the little woman's signalling."

Cooling turned to find that in the split second Caswell had become engrossed in conversation with the red-haired lady who kept one's best things in the drawing room. Brent was pushing his way towards the little woman, who appeared to be the one with the parade-ground voice.

The Colonel hovered in the doorway, as though making up his mind about some advanced strategy. Cooling looked away before the old soldier caught his eye, edged further into the room and came up against an attractive young woman with large brown eyes and the look of one who is out of her depth.

"We haven't met," he plunged.

She smiled, a hint of fatigue around the eyes. "I'm afraid I know hardly anyone. We've only just moved into the village."

"Snap. I'm only here for the holiday. Cooling's the name. My mother lives in The Flats—Heath Corner."

"Oh," recognition dawning. "That's just across the road from us. We've moved into Pine Copse End. My name's Sybil. Sybil Gotterson."

"Hallo." Their hands touched. "And do you like it here in sleepy Tilt?"

She grinned. "Too soon to tell, but I think so. I've never lived in the country before, so it's all new and quite exciting."

"I was looking at your house yesterday," he rushed on, quickly, not wanting to see her slip away. "It seems an interesting place. My mother was telling me that it's got quite a history. Actually I believe we saw you walking over the recreation ground. You've got a little girl, haven't you?"

"Yes, Helen. It's all been a great load of excitement for her. The new house, Christmas. She's only two and a half." Her brow creased, "What did your mother tell you about the house?"

"Ah," he laughed. "The village legend. The haunted house." As he said it, Cooling saw her shy away, not a dramatic movement: maybe not even a movement of her body at all. It was as though she was wincing, some hurt passing near her.

"It is rather scary," the twitch of a smile, unsure, uncertain whether he was being jokey.

"As my mother says, villages need their legends, their fantasies."

"Quite honestly, it's the only thing that bothers me, but perhaps you think I'm being stupid. Do you believe in ghosts?"

She was perfectly serious, and embarrassed by even a half-admission of fear.

"Why? Have you really got a ghost? Have you seen it?"

"I don't know," another nervous laugh, trying to be bright and jolly. She's isolated, thought Cooling. She's alone in this. "There are strange noises. My husband laughs at me. Thinks I'm a bit stupid about it. Do you believe in ghosts?" she asked again.

"Nobody can deny the paranormal. I have my own beliefs about such things. It must be very difficult for you—coming to a house with that kind of reputation. Particularly if you're blessed with an imagination."

"You do think I'm being silly. My husband says it's imagination."

"Not at all. I've just said, one cannot deny the paranormal. Whether the ghosts exist outside oneself is a different matter."

He saw that her eyes were being drawn away from his, expectantly over his shoulder, then from behind him he heard the voice—"Are you meeting lots of people, Angel? Having a good time?"

Cooling turned.

Somehow he had not expected it to be so normal, so ordinary, this meeting with the man who had engrossed him on paper for the past few days. Maybe, he considered later, he had wanted some dramatic setting, not these conventional middle-class surroundings with the Colonel's trophies of war and the comfortable people.

He was also surprised that he liked the man instantly: shortish, powerfully built, relaxed, the face friendly, open, but for the eyes, which held a cold spot deep in the blue.

"This is my husband, Mr. Cooling. Joseph, Mr. Cooling's mother lives opposite us in The Flats."

"So?" The smile widened. "I've just met your mother, Mr. Cooling. You must meet her also, Angel. She says you must go to tea with her and take Helen."

"She'd love that." Cooling put out his hand, feeling that with the firmness of Gotterson's grip a circle had been completed.

Werewolf stood before him, stripped from the murky shadows of the reports, an ordinary man. He even found himself searching his face, trying to detect an immediate likeness between Gotterson and the man Maitland-Wood dearly wished to believe was his father. He found none.

"Do you think she really would?"

Sybil Gotterson sounded as though she was almost frantic to make friends: to be accepted. Did she know about her husband's past? Had he told her of the night when, as a child, an SS officer had taken him by the hand and led him away from the concrete tomb? Did she know that he was Werewolf? The child in the Hitler Youth, decorated with the Iron Cross? Or the only son of Reich Minister Doktor Goebbels?

"I'm sure," he said gently, the mind busy with queries: did she share in his politics, whatever those politics were?

"Let's go and find her." Joseph Gotterson put out his hand, smoothing the material of her dress, on her shoulder, a movement of great gentleness.

Cooling nodded. "Why not?"

"I am making a lot of friends," Gotterson said, smiling back over his shoulder. "We are already asked to dinner with two people. You'll have to get your new diary out before we go home, Angel."

Cooling felt again that instinct he had followed from the start: the stupidity of it all, the sense that through all the paperwork he had been swimming against the tide of reason. Then he remembered what people had said about being on the clandestine side—learning to trust very few individuals; never taking anybody at his face value; always looking behind, at the paperwork, the final answer in the algebra.

He knew later that the meeting had, in many ways, been a disappointment. Werewolf had assumed such historic importance in his mind, had been such a spectre, overshadowing him, that he expected to imme-

diately detect some strain of evil, even an obvious and
unpleasant habit in the man. Instead he actually liked
him, finding his normality at odds with the image.

They came across his mother in the hall, and for a
few minutes he was cut off from the Gottersons, but-
tonholed by the Colonel, who wanted to tell him how
much they enjoyed the little bridge parties with his
mother.

"Wonderful woman," he puffed, a boring old war-
horse. "Backbone, that's what she's got. Charming.
Plays bridge well. I'll say that for her. Plays damned
well. Always glad to have her as my partner. Better
than Dotty, my wife. Too scatterbrained to play well."

When he escaped, the Gottersons were over on the
far side of the room again, and he felt it would be un-
wise to push matters further.

"She's bringing the little girl to tea next week," his
mother said, taking care not to slur as they walked
slowly back over the recreation ground. "They seem
nice, your Mr. and Mrs. Gotterson." She leaned against
him.

"They do." His mind already leaping ahead to
Steph's arrival.

"Any special instructions?" It was asked with an air
of innocence.

He switched back to the here and now. "Only if anything boils up; if she's really frightened—she's nervous
in that house—or if they suggest dinner. Get in touch if
I can be brought in."

She stopped walking, turning her head towards his face, the light, cold wind tugging at her coat and making his ears tingle. Over in Scholars Road he saw the Gottersons' car slowing at the drive to Pine Copse End.

"Is it really something serious?" her face troubled.

Worrying about the child, he thought. She always worries about children. "It's probably nothing. I mean that. Probably nothing at all. Keep your ear to the ground, though, Mum."

She started forward, slowly, nodding her head as though she really knew everything.

When they reached the entrance to Heath Corner, Steph's Mini was in the driveway. She was early.

14

In spite of all Mrs. Cooling's charm, Steph remained immovable. She was so sorry to be a nusiance; she had managed to get coffee on the way down; no, if Mrs. Cooling didn't mind she really had to get back to London.

"Looks jittery to me," his mother said as he picked up his case in the hall. "Try to get her to let you drive, dear. Nice-looking girl, smart, but there's something wrong. You two haven't been silly, have you?"

Cooling smiled to himself, a mother's first thought was of getting a girl pregnant. One is cocooned in the mores of one's youth, unless you break free, and even then you revert to type if your own flesh and blood is at risk.

Steph would not talk at first. "Later, I just want to

be with you," she said, refusing to let him drive until, on the far side of the Guildford bypass, he insisted that she slow down and pull into a lay-by. There was a fair amount of traffic about, British Rail having refused trains on this Boxing Day, and they sat, still and quiet, rocked occasionally by the wash of other people's cars. Then she began to cry, leaning her head on his shoulder. "I've been such an idiot." It did not sound like self-pity. "Will you hate me?" The question posed more to herself than him.

"Come on." He passed an arm around her shoulders. "Tell me all about it," deep down dreading what might come.

When she finally began to get the story out, he went chill, shuddering at the implications.

It had happened in New York. "Have you heard of a French politician called Maubert?" she asked.

He had. Alain Maubert was a junior minister, young, thrusting and with a powerful reputation. His enemies called him The Priest, for he was a fanatic over the question of his country's morals in general and his colleagues' in particular. His marriage was often held up by the far right Catholic press as an outstanding example of the family triumphing against the commonly accepted morals of the day. He was also regarded as that most rare man, the honest politician, though his enemies, and there were many, whispered that, when finally this paragon of virtue cracked, the scandal would rock the foundations of government.

"The firm's doing a deal with the French, a boring new computer process. I met him at a reception—he was in New York for a UN meeting." She blew her nose, hard, and took a deep breath. "It was so stupid. He's devoted to his wife and the principles people sneer at—well, they're real. Yet . . ."

"You went to bed with him." Cooling felt intense pain, even fury for a second: with her, Maubert, himself, her firm pulling her out of Berlin.

She nodded. "I didn't know about you. Not really, so please don't be angry."

"Go on," calm to the brink of a storm.

"It really was stupid. We got cut off from everybody else. We had dinner together. We talked politics, and his wife, God he went on about his wife, and the children. We drank a lot and I went back to his room for coffee. Then it just happened. Oh, Vincent, afterwards he was terrible. I've never seen a man like it. It was as though he was a girl of sixteen that's just lost her virginity to some idiot. He pleaded with me to tell nobody. It was embarrassing."

"What's the problem, then?" The iron in his soul.

She hesitated for a long time, fiddling with her handkerchief. "You are with Dan Hardwicke's lot, aren't you?"

"Why?" the apprehension tightening his stomach.

"I know I'm not supposed to ask, but I need to know. You are with his lot?"

He nodded.

"The day I got back to the office after New York—
the day before you rang—a woman telephoned me. She
asked if she could meet me after I'd finished work. Said
she had a proposition for me. Work of national importance, she said. Government work. I tried to put her
off, but she insisted."

"So you went with her and she showed you the photographs." It was the oldest scenario in the business;
though in reverse. "What was it? Industrial espio-
nage?"

She shook her head. "No, she was genuine. Government. Said I'd done a good job in New York. I didn't
know what she meant at first. Until, like you say, she
showed me the photographs. To be quite honest I was
more worried about Alain. He'd been in such a sweat.
But she told me that he'd taken it very well. Then she
asked me to do it again. For the government."

"Yes, I know the form." He saw the repercussions
and the endless chain of possibilities spreading out like
a bleak polar landscape. "They call it recruiting for the
Ladies' Auxiliary Unit. What did you tell her?"

"I said that I didn't think I could."

"And?"

"She said they had the pictures. It would be a pity
for me to be involved in a scandal."

"That's bluff. They've sanctified Maubert and those
pictures are only good for one thing."

"Sanctified?"

"It's what they call it. They've made him holy, separated him. Blackmailed him."

"On Christmas night—last night: it seems ages ago—she telephoned me. She said it was essential that we meet straight after the holiday, because they were probably going to take action against the Frenchman—that's what she said, the Frenchman. She said that they had the photographs and some recordings. It was up to me which they used. I'm not a prude, but I'd lose my job even in our great permissive, understanding age. The chairman's a one hundred per cent super Baptist. Besides, there are parents and things. And you."

"So you've said you'll do it?" He stared blankly through the windshield, knowing he was disgusted with himself for even thinking it.

"Don't be bloody silly," she flared, red flushes down her cheeks. "I'm supposed to meet her on Monday. I had to tell you and I had to talk to you. Nobody else, Vincent, so for God's sake treat me like an adult. I want to know what I should do."

"What'd you tell your parents?"

"I said a friend was ill. In London. I left in the early hours and drove to London."

"Then you phoned me and drove straight on down. You'll let me take us back to town. Or, better still, some hotel where we can stay and think. They'll probably have your place wired by now anyway, the whole *son et lumière*."

She looked puzzled. "Can you do anything?"

"If you're asking if I'm high enough up the ladder to meddle, the answer's no. On the other hand I think that there are those who'll be only too glad to do me a favour." Only too glad, he said to himself. The whole thing was a Mexican standoff, a three-way split where no one party could win. Aloud he asked, "Did the woman give you a name?"

"Sanders. Hilary Sanders."

"Of the bloody river, I suppose."

He got out of the car, made her shift over, and took the wheel. Within ten minutes she was asleep and did not stir again until he pulled up, well away from London, at the Randolph Hotel in Oxford. But by then he knew the shadows were with him once more.

15

He spotted the yellow ex-Post Office van just as they joined the M4 Motorway; then, again, at intervals along the route up to the Oxford turnout, where its place was taken by an elderly Dormobile.

There was nothing unusual about either of the vehicles, nor could Cooling have provided direct evidence that they were shadows, though his instinct left him in little doubt.

That they were more or less friendly—in the widest possible sense—was borne out by the appearance of the van across the road from the Randolph in Beaumont Street soon after their arrival. After all, he knew they were watching his back.

There was no problem about getting a room; they both had luggage (Steph had not removed hers from the car since leaving Norfolk) and booked in as Mr. and Mrs. Cooling.

It was now late afternoon and Steph, having slept for the entire journey, was still dopey and tired. She tried to bring up the Maubert business several times, but Cooling turned her away from it, gently telling her that she must not worry. Tonight was for R & R; tomorrow he would have another go at her to get the facts straight.

They both bathed and changed, watched television and ate—a light meal of inevitable cold turkey and salad—in their room. Before sleep they made love once, in a tired, quiet way which did not call for athletics.

The next morning he took her for a walk in Christ Church Meadows.

"Maubert," he said, breaking the embargo. "There are things I have to know. Nothing to do with jealousy, I promise you that. I have to know how deeply you're involved with these people."

She nodded, tight-lipped as though she did not altogether believe him.

"For instance, you said that at the reception—when you met Maubert—the two of you were cut off from the others. How come?"

"It just happened."

"Steph, these things don't just happen. Think back to the start. Who introduced you?"

"Our head of advertising."

"How many in your party?"

"The chairman, my boss, head of advertising, and myself." She ticked them off on her fingers. Her boss was the managing director of the British office.

"You hadn't met Maubert before?"

"I'd seen him. He was part of a team that came over to discuss the project—the one with the French: the boring computer processing."

"So you'd seen plenty of letters written to him?"

"Not directly to him."

"And you knew his reputation?"

"Naturally."

"Was there any problem with the deal? The project?"

"Vague worries in financial areas. Nothing difficult."

"And the American trip was not really concerned with the French project?"

"No. The meeting was accidental." She brushed a hand lightly through her hair as if trying to get rid of something which was tangled in it.

"Tell me what your head of advertising said when he introduced you."

"I think he said something like, 'Good, Maubert's here, let's soften him up.' We both went over and after a while Jimmy, our head of advertising, left us alone."

"Jimmy who?"

"James Kentish."

"Did you feel particularly deserted by your people?"

They had fallen into step, walking close to one another: lovers or academics.

"Not really. Alain Maubert was charming. I enjoyed talking with him."

"None of his team stayed around?"

"No."

"Where was all this?"

"The Waldorf Towers. We were all staying there."

"Big and stuffy. Who mentioned dinner?"

"I think he did. No, I said I'd have to go and eat."

"Were you giving him the come-on?"

"Oh, Vincent, do I have to . . . ?"

"Yes, you do. It doesn't matter. Really it doesn't."

"I was bloody bored in New York. I suppose I was just starting to realise how much I was missing you. Confused between Berlin and you. Yes, I gave him a kind of come-on. But only for dinner. Alain Maubert's reputation is incorruptible."

"Did the possibility of sex cross your mind?"

"I don't think so."

"Were there other opportunities in New York?"

She slowed down, her arm resting on his. "Jimmy made a pass. I wasn't interested and he went off, meek as a lamb."

"And Maubert reacted to your need to eat?"

"Straight away."

"Did you eat in the hotel?"

"Yes."

So they had been in the hotel all the time: plenty of opportunity for an ad lib operation.

"What did you talk about?"

She shrugged. "France, England, the politics of ter-
rorism, his wife and kids. Me."

"What about you?"

"Usual stuff. Background; schooldays; parents."

"Lovers?"

"No."

"What did you drink?"

"I think he had a half bottle of something red—I
don't know what: he was eating beef. I had a half of
Moët & Chandon."

"You have much at the reception?"

"Not a great deal, no."

"Can you remember what you were both drinking
there?"

"I had some vodka. I'm not sure about him."

"Brandy, liqueurs, after the meal?"

"Yes, we both had one brandy each."

"And who suggested his room for coffee?"

"He did."

"Definitely?"

"Yes."

"And you still didn't think he was after fun and
games?"

"No, I didn't. His reputation hung around him like a
bloody shroud." For the first time she laughed. "I got
the surprise of my life."

They had completed a wide sweep and were coming
back towards Merton Street. A young don with his wife
and two small children passed them, the man deep in

conversation with the woman, the children circling them like small, noisy sheep dogs. Cooling thought briefly of Werewolf's wife and little Helen; saw them stumping over the recreation ground at Tilt, Sybil sweeping the girl up in her arms, then taking the dog's lead and letting her husband swing the child round, his hands under her arms. From his mother's window he had heard her squeals of glee.

"This isn't a question of morbid fascination," he told Steph. "I don't like being your father confessor and your lover, but it is important. What happened?"

Her lips tightened and she looked away. "You want all the gory details? Like how he groped me and whether he undressed me and was he good?"

"Not really, but you'll have to tell me—at least about the pillow chat; and about his first approach."

She gave a frustrated sigh. "He just came over and kissed me."

"And you responded?"

"Yes."

"How did he seem when he did this?"

"I don't follow."

"Did you think he was drunk?"

"I thought it was out of character. Christ, it *was* out of character. I was amazed."

"Did you think he was a little high?"

The answer took a moment or two coming. She had to take it slowly and seriously. "Just before," she was thinking hard, "just before he came over and kissed me, he seemed unsteady. I remember that when he stood up he had to hold on to the chair. He said, 'Whoops,' or something like that."

Cooling's throat felt dry. "I'm sorry, Steph. Was he agile? Had the drink taken its toll, I mean set him up, and then taken away the performance? I'm sorry, love, you have to answer."

She looked away. "Oh, Christ," then, sadly, "Yes, very agile. Very potent."

He thought she was going to cry again. "You need help," lacing his fingers with hers. "I'm trying to give it. It all happened in the bedroom?"

"Yes."

"Now the pillow talk."

She looked desperately miserable. "During or after?"

"All of it. You can remember if you try."

"I think I've indicated some of it to you. He was very warm and loving."

"He spoke in French?"

"Yes."

"Endearments?"

She nodded.

"Anything out of the ordinary?"

Her brow creased once more as a small memory returned.

"In the restaurant he was calling me Stephanie. In bed he called me . . . I can't remember, it was odd . . . Dine, I think it was."

"Dine?"

"Yes, I'm sure."

"And afterwards."

"That was strange. Even more strange thinking back. We lay there and I smoked a cigarette. He went on touching me for a while, then suddenly he changed."

"Suddenly?"

"Well, maybe it wasn't so sudden. Perhaps it came on over five, ten, minutes. His whole tone changed. He started saying, 'Oh, God. Oh, my God.' And then he began to apologise and accuse himself. He got up and told me to get dressed. He said that he had betrayed his wife and didn't know what had come over him. He didn't blame me at all. It was him, and how this had never happened before. Silly and melodramatic. I told you, like a sixteen-year-old virgin."

"He got quite hysterical?"

"That's an understatement."

"Last question. Can you remember seeing anyone, when you went to his room, that you saw again when you left?"

She had her thinking face on again. "The bellboy in the lift. We went up to his floor—the seventh. I was on the eighth. It was the same boy. Well, you know what I mean, he was a middle-aged little man really."

"Okay, love. If this Hilary Sanders gets in touch on Monday, tell her you don't want to know. I'll try to get her off your back. I'll phone you if I have anything definite." He turned to face her. "We won't talk about it again. That was then and now is now. After Monday we'll see if we've got a future. Be careful, though, in your flat and on the phone."

She looked as though she was going to ask another question, and then changed her mind. He wished that she had spoken, but did not want to press.

Most of the shops were open again after the holiday, and they joined the Saturday crowds. Oxford had changed much since he had last been there, the new grey concrete and glass shops springing up and pressing in on the old remembered city like scar tissue. It made Cooling afraid, and conscious of his own rapid progress towards the mystic age of forty: the new and the young, he was told, begin to encroach on your ideas and memories once you have crossed that line.

They went down to Blackwells and browsed among the books, and he found what he wanted quite quickly —*The Political Who's Who of Europe*. Steph was looking through the novels, glancing at blurbs and then rejecting them.

He found Maubert and ran his finger down the biography: *m. 1958 Claudine Félicie* (*nee Cranbon*). Claudine? Dine? He raised his eyebrows, closing the book and returning it to the shelf. Dine? A diminutive of Claudine? A pet name? Steph was with him again. She had bought a paperback of Le Carré's *The Looking-Glass War*.

"That's about a cock-up as well," he said.

She clung to his arm as they walked back along the Broad, and he felt old enough, and conservative enough, to think most seriously about asking her to marry him. He thought she would if he only asked. He would not be popular with Maitland-Wood, that was certain. For a fraction he thought it might be worth it for that alone.

They checked out of the hotel before noon on Sunday, but stayed on for lunch. Then, leaving Steph with the car, Cooling went to a telephone box and rang the house off St. James's. Gibbs was back and came, reluctantly, to the phone.

"I want to see the DD first thing in the morning," he told Gibbs.

"I don't know if that can be managed." Gibbs sounded as if Christmas had not agreed with him.

"It'll have to be managed. It's urgent. If he can't make it in the morning, I need to see him tonight. I cannot carry on until I've seen him."

"I don't think you're in a position to dictate . . ."

"Just tell him. I think he'll know what I'm talking about. I'll be back around six."

He hung up, the whole picture of the New York business quite clear in his head now, with the repercussions looming large over his shoulder.

The yellow van stayed with them all the way back to London, and he said goodbye to Steph on the steps of the house in which she had her flat.

"Be in touch tomorrow," he told her cheerily. "Don't worry, you're much loved."

He got into the house around quarter to six. Gibbs was in the hall and Greg sat on a chair near the study door.

"He's waiting for you now." Gibbs nodded towards the study. "It'd better be good, though; you've taken him away from the bosom of his family."

"I think he probably took me away from mine." He winked at Greg, tapped at the study door and went in.

16

Maitland-Wood was not dressed for town. He sat near
the electric fire, his suede shoes almost touching the
bars: old grey slacks and some kind of loose woollen
jacket. There was a file on his knee and a large cigar
between his lips.

"You've met him, then, Vincent?" he said without
looking up.

"Werewolf? Yes."

"And?"

"And nothing yet. I haven't completed the evaluation."

"Then why the hell have you brought me all the way
in from the country? I can't see you in the morning,
I've got a meeting with the Minister at nine-thirty?"

"Oh, I'm sorry." Cooling sat down across the fire

from him, leaning forward. "I thought I'd made it plain to Tony. I'd have met you at five tomorrow morning if you'd wanted."

The Deputy Director eyed him with distaste. "What's the urgency, then?"

"I think you know."

"I'm not a mind-reader."

"Earlier this month there was a black operation in New York—I presume our American section."

"Really?"

"I suspect that it was an ad lib job, done on the wing. The subject was Alain Maubert."

"Oh yes." Maitland-Wood smiled.

"I suspect it was ad libbed because there was a lady concerned who is not a member of the Ladies' Auxiliary."

"And what's this got to do with you? You're an evaluator and, as you would doubtless tell me if I suggested it to you, sanctification's not really your line."

"Apparently the news has been laid on the subject: and I gather it's also been laid on the girl. You have a talent scout for the ladies with the work name Hilary Sanders."

"A good girl." He drew in smoke from the cigar and looked quite pleased with himself. "Yes, as you've brought it up, the Maubert thing went well. We've been offering him all sorts of people: Paris, London, all over the place. Then he takes a shine to an unknown."

"With a little bit of help from the wine waiter. I don't know what you'd use nowadays but it did the job, removed the mental and spiritual obstacles."

"Not just the wine waiter, or whoever they used. Naturally we had assistance from the Americans. No poaching. It was all very slick, and also makeshift. They fixed up two rooms, his and hers, in less than an hour. But, with respect, I fail to see what this had to do with Werewolf."

"The girl you used."

"Yes, Vincent?" A schoolmaster waiting for a confession. Maitland-Wood might have made a good headmaster. A small private prep school. There was nothing State-aided about him.

"She's a friend of mine."

"Then all I can say is you should choose your friends more carefully. I didn't think you were one for tarts, Vincent."

Cooling very much wanted to hit him. "It's quite possible that I shall marry her."

"Good God." The Deputy Director's jaw dropped, as good a piece of simulation as Cooling had seen for a long time.

"She's not a tart, sir. We were apart; she was bored. It happens even in your own stratosphere. It's not an unknown phenomenon."

"No, I had heard." It was impossible to tell if he was being amusing. "And your Miss—what's her name?"

"Bishop. Stephanie Bishop."

"Yes, your Miss Bishop's come to you and told all, I suppose."

"Hilary Sanders put the boot in on Christmas night. Miss Bishop landed in Tilt on Boxing Day."

"Penitent, I trust."

"She told me everything."

"And you forgave her. How nice. You must have done, otherwise you wouldn't be here now. *Te absolve* and all that."

"It was understandable in the circumstances."

Maitland-Wood ran his hands over the grey flannel covering his thighs. "You would like me to call the dogs off, that it?"

"It would seem to be the best thing for all concerned?"

The Deputy Director nodded, his hands still smoothing the thighs, like a woman at an old-fashioned washtub. "My dear fellow, of course. You're quite right. It wouldn't be the thing for you to be married to one of our ladies, would it? I'm glad you had the sense to come straight to me." The hand with the cigar made an ecclesiastical gesture in the air. "Pity, though. Bishop's a good name for that kind of work. She won't run loose on you again, will she?"

"I think it's highly unlikely."

"Don't think any more about it, then. A shame, though. It was always thought that Stephanie Bishop had great potential. The talent spotters have kept an eye on her since Berlin. A girl like that with a job

which takes her into sensitive areas—well, a godsend."
He shrugged, an unpleasant movement. "I need not
tell you that it was not altogether an accident that she
was placed close to the French gentleman in New
York."

"Manipulation's always been a strong point with
your people, hasn't it?"

"I must say they are rather good at placing people
who don't know they're being placed."

Cooling knew that it was the closing of the trap, the
completing of the circuit. They had his soul now and
could lead him by the nose to perdition.

"So what about Werewolf, Vincent? Are we going to
run him to earth?"

"I don't know about that yet." The picture was conjured straight and bloody; Gotterson with his wife and
child running in terror across the recreation ground at
Tilt, the hounds baying at their heels, the child's
screams floating up to where he stood, looking on, at
his mother's window. "I'll have the evaluation done in
a few days. Then you can decide."

"Then we can both decide."

"All right, we'll both decide. But I'll let you worry
about fascist Michael Rivers and Robin Chilton's new
book."

"I do worry about them. It's because of people like
that we're involved to this extent. The Minister . . ."

"Is seeing ghosts under his bed. Does he see Marxist
ghosts as well, or are they all confined to the ludicrous

possibilities like Werewolf?" Cooling shook his head. "You're all crazy. The notion hardly holds water. You're jumping at shadows."

"He exists, Vincent. He existed in the past. Maybe he is not a threat. But the Minister wants him quietly removed and I want to know the truth about him."

Cooling felt his shoulders hunch forward. He almost quoted Pontius Pilate—What is truth?—but stopped himself in time. Later, he reflected that Maitland-Wood was a natural for Pilate.

On the Sunday night at Pine Copse End, Sybil Gotterson woke, cold but sweating, certain that she could hear once more the sound of feet on the stairs and across the uncarpeted landing.

This time she was terrified. Two things had occurred on the Sunday. The carving knife had gone missing after lunch (it had not yet been found), and when she went to draw the bedroom curtains she clearly heard the noise of great wings from the trees.

She lay, almost frozen with fright, as her ears strained for the tiny footsteps, while Joseph, at her side, breathed peacefully.

17

Adolf Hitler approached the ragged line of uniformed boys in the Reich Chancellery garden. Surrounded by his officers and the entourage of his court, the Führer now looked a pathetic caricature of the man who, for five years, wielded the might of Nazi Germany against the rest of Europe.

His walk had become shambollic, one arm held in front of his body, against the flapping greatcoat, crooked and stiff as though paralysed; the face that of an old man, creased and lined, collapsing in on itself; the eyes pouched and glazed—haunted—and the skin texture already bearing the marks of decay.

There were stiff salutes, and the Führer began to pass along the line of boy soldiers, his face occasionally coming alive as he spoke to individuals.

In front of one small boy his old familiar charm seemed momentarily resurrected as he put out an arm to pat the child's shoulder, caressing his neck and face: an action which was both pathetic and moving.

The occasion was Hitler's fifty-sixth birthday: April 20, 1945. He had only ten days to live.

The picture flickered, the screen going clear as Cooling leaned forward to switch off the video machine and rewind the tape. Already he had gone over the sequence a dozen times. Still photographs of it, and other, nameless things littered his desk, together with books, papers and files. It was the last film ever taken of Adolf Hitler: the investiture in the Chancellery garden which Shallow (the SS Corporal Schmidt) claimed to have seen; while the lad, whose cheek Hitler fondled, was the boy whom Moonlight (the SS Major Kritter) ordered to be taken to General Mohnke's nearby bunker.

Around the old Reich Chancellery, in the heart of Berlin, several of these deep shelters had been built: the final command posts, and tombs, of the Nazi party. For almost a week now, Cooling had sifted through what evidence remained, from those concrete bolt-holes and their occupants, in an attempt to bring reason to the question which obsessed the Deputy Director.

The facts, such as they were, remained available to everybody. The story had been told time and time again, in some ways becoming a legend: in books, on film, television and radio. There were still puzzles, of course; some pieces were missing; but the general sweep of events was clear.

Almost too clear, he thought, leaning back in his chair. The whole panorama of the Second World War was so vast, so dramatic, that no one person could contain it all. Yet the end of the one man who had been its axis still haunted the minds of thinkers and historians.

He stood up, going to the window, looking down upon Whitehall. A group of students, long-haired, happy, went past heading towards the Cenotaph. When those kids studied history, he smiled, what did they make of it? Did they ask, How could one man so change the destiny of Europe?

The very fact that one man had been able to commit the atrocious acts of dictatorship was the reason Cooling was there, sitting in this room, cudgelling his brains over that other man who was Werewolf.

The film he had just watched was shot at a moment when the war had reached its conclusion. The Russian armies, taking their time, circled the city of Berlin, poised to smash inwards.

"He who rules Berlin rules Europe," Cooling spoke aloud, trying to remember whether he was quoting a politician or a soldier.

Hitler had gone from that sad little parade back to his bunker, cut off from reality, playing an obscene war game, wrapped in paranoia and refusing to believe the war was lost. By the time the birthday was over, his old comrades, many of whom had served with him through the rebuilding of Germany, had left Berlin and the bunker for the last time.

"Christ." He sat down, staring at the piled desk, his mind roving over the intense atmosphere which must have built inside the thick cold walls of those grim shelters, where the Führer remained with the final characters of the drama—the few soldiers and servants; the doctors, like Stumpfegger and Haas; the Generals: Krebs, Burgdorf and Weidling whose photographs were on the desk (but Cooling could not have put the correct name to each picture); the adjutants and secretaries; his mistress, Eva Braun (the servants treated her like a cipher, calling her "EB"); the brown eminence, Reichsleiter Martin Bormann; and the stunted, clubfoot Reich Minister, Paul Joseph Goebbels, together with his wife, Magda, and their six children.

He was depressed, as he had been all week, the claustrophobic sense of the bunker constantly in his mind, so tightly had he shut himself away with these particular ghosts. There were times when he could almost hear the gentle roar of the bunker's air conditioning; and the changes of mood, the viciousness, rages and tears whispered back from the terse reports and written dialogue of history.

Yet, all the time, he thought about the boy deep in General Mohnke's shelter, who was only removed after Kritter had come down, on April 30, to say that Hitler was dead. He wondered about the things left unsaid in

that odd interrogation reported by Cobra. Did Major
Kritter tell them how Hitler had died? Of the suicide
pact with Eva Braun? Of their marriage the day before? What did they eat down there? Did they give the
boy brandy to calm him against the distant explosions?
Did Kritter talk about the burning of the bodies in the
Chancellery garden, as the Russians drew nearer and
their shells screamed down around the Brandenburg
Gate? Did they know that the Red Flag was already
hoisted on the Reichstag building?

If one believed Cobra's report—if one believed Shallow—Major Kritter was seen leaving the Chancellery
garden twenty-four hours later with the boy. The time
was right, for that night, May 1, was the night of the
mass breakout, left until the last minute, for the Russians were by then nearly upon them. For many it was
left too late.

There were no new clues though, and, for all he
could tell, no way of knowing what happened to the
boy, so young and bemused in the film, between leaving Mohnke's bunker and the abandonment of the
Führer-bunker. Was it indeed him? Or was the little
figure in reality Helmut, only son of Paul Joseph and
Magda Goebbels? Which one of them was Joseph Gotterson, alive and well, living in a haunted house in
Surrey?

By now Cooling knew that there was only one way
to find out. It was all a question of ghosts, he thought:
ghosts from the past and from the present; shadows in

the mind; fears in the heart; ghosts, if one thought of Maitland-Wood's mind, of the future.

The historians argued over the evidence of Hitler's death. Did he shoot himself or, as the Russians maintained, take poison? Had the Russians really found his body, and that of Eva Braun? Nobody, until Maitland-Wood's meddling, has ever questioned the identity of the small body that was Goebbels' son. While he still considered the whole matter improbable, Cooling now knew why it so obsessed the Deputy Director; for it was a fascinating problem, incredible and absorbing.

There was little doubt that Kritter had left the bunker with a child: they had been identified in Spain only a couple of weeks later; then in South America. Cooling, like his principal, desperately wanted to know who that child was, if for no other reason than to satisfy curiosity, for it could be left to others to prove plots and dangers.

Had Kritter taken the boy to the Führer-bunker and hidden him away until the horrors were past? Until the last farewells were said, the hideous poisoning of the children done, and the parents dead and burning, like Hitler and Eva, in the garden? Or had he been kept for but a short time, then poisoned like a small dog, to be dressed in Helmut Goebbels' pyjamas and placed beside the little girls while young Helmut, holding fast the Major's hand, was hurried from the sickening scene of death?

Incredible, absorbing, fantastic and, possibly, pointless like all acts of war. What was it that Eva Braun had said to Albert Speer, Hitler's Minister of War Production, during their last meeting? "Why do so many people have to be killed? And it's all for nothing." How many people had echoed that sentiment down the ages and into our own century? From then to here, and now among the terrorists, or freedom fighters, and their victims.

The chances of some deep-seated plot, he thought, were remote; for it made no sense. But very little of what went on in the bunker during those last days of hallucination made sense.

He picked up the telephone and rang through to the Deputy Director's office. Yes, the drawling lady told him, the DD would see him now.

"I thought you might want a verbal evaluation before I get down to the paperwork," he told Maitland-Wood.

They sat on opposite sides of the functional desk, pictures of the Queen and Prince Philip smiling from the wall, between the metal filing cabinet and the safe; rain spotting the two large windows, which seemed to hang on the Deputy Director's shoulders; the room baffled from noise, a teacup of superior design on the desk. A Prince Consort, thought Cooling. Crown Derby. Expensive.

"Come to fence with me before you commit yourself, eh?"

He was in his working clothes again: the Civil Servant or Harley Street man, ready to rush to the Minister, or press the buttons for a hundred nefarious operations.

"Not fence, but maybe think aloud."

"Your young woman all right?" a suspect sneer dribbling from his lips. Put him in a toga and he would be like a Roman just before the fall. He had about him a sense of being part of the long sunset: a type, a class, hanging on but in decline.

"Thank you, fine," glancing quickly at his watch, remembering that he was to see her tonight: the first time for three days.

"You've decided, then?" covering his eagerness with a languid hand to the mouth.

"I think so."

"Try me."

"It is possible, just possible, that a substitution took place. But there can be no proof of it. Nor can there be proof that such an action was instigated by any of the senior people in the Führer-bunker. In fact the opposite is suggested."

"And that is your considered opinion?"

He nodded.

"Construe." Like a supercilious schoolmaster.

"I will grant that both Moonlight and Werewolf existed, and that Werewolf still exists. The evidence in your trace reports is overwhelming. I will also grant that they both probably left the bunker systems on the night of May 1, 1945. But we cannot rule out the possibility that Werewolf did not come from the bunker at all. There is no concrete evidence to link the boy, who was seen first in Spain with Moonlight—Kritter—as one who was in the bunker."

"It is likely that he was, though," Maitland-Wood said, nodding, taking the matter quietly.

"It's probable," said Cooling. "Also, if the boy did come from the bunker he was either a boy soldier or young Goebbels. However, I can see no reason for believing in a plot to provide Nazism with a Prince Regent in hiding, and under training for the big event of the future."

"Good. Go on."

"If we are to believe your subject Shallow's story about being instructed to remove the boy after the investiture; and if we are to believe that this was the first step in a contingency plan, we are in deep water. The dates are all wrong for a start. In Shallow's interrogation, he maintains that Moonlight spent some time with Hitler and Goebbels on the night before the investiture; and that it was during the actual parade that he fingered the boy."

"Yes?"

"We know the parade took place on Hitler's birthday. The twentieth. At that point all the evidence shows that Hitler had not yet quite made up his mind to stay in Berlin, and that he still would not believe the war finished. Nor did Goebbels have any plans for bringing his wife and children into the bunkers.

The Deputy Director chuckled, "Yes, but they were all at sixes and sevens. Almost everybody knew the war was lost."

"Yet the Führer forbade anyone to say it aloud."

"It did not stop them thinking it, though." His head tilted back in a gesture of arrogance. "Including Hitler."

"True." Cooling steadied himself. Take it gently, he cautioned. "If we're looking for some plot, we surely have to consider it as motivating from either Hitler or Goebbels. The Führer's later statements indicate that he felt everything was lost, finished. In the end, both Hitler and Goebbels were screaming for blood: the destruction of Germany. If the Party was finished, then the people it claimed to lead would be shattered with it. Hitler constantly said that Germany wasn't good enough. It should go to the wall. At his wedding party he said that National Socialism was finished and would never revive."

"Goebbels didn't think it was finished," Maitland-Wood said calmly. "He said Germany had to be destroyed so that it could be reconstructed. He meant also that the Party would be reconstructed."

The rain was coming down heavily now, audible on the windows, the sky darkening outside and the lights going on along Whitehall.

"Maybe." Cooling squinted as Maitland-Wood switched on his desk lamp. There was no need, for the tubular lights in the ceiling burned all day. The desk

lamp made Cooling think of old American movies, with
police giving the third degree: or the Gestapo, Hollywood style, with their rubber hoses and torture hinted
at. "Yes, I thought Goebbels had hoped for the future.
It was one of the reasons he gave for his suicide—'In
the vanguard of the peoples it is we who carry the
torch'—but it's unlikely that he would have chosen his
son as the candidate. He didn't even like Helmut very
much: found him slow and stupid. He preferred Helga,
the eldest girl. If Helmut was to be saved for the future, it's also unlikely that Magda would've agreed."

The Deputy Director grunted. "One dead, all dead."

"Something like that. 'The world without Hitler will
have no room for them,' is how she put it."

"You consider that she'd have to be part of the plot?
That they would have to seek her agreement?"

"I'd have thought so. The Führer-bunker wasn't very
big, you know. The evidence suggests that the Goebbels family spent their last hours together. She'd have
to know. Anyway, it's generally considered that she
played a vital part in the murder of the children."

"That is an interesting aspect, isn't it?" He could
have been speaking of some scheme to redecorate his
office. "Who done it?"

"Interesting, yes, and loathsome."

"Come, Vincent. Six children. Think of the thousands
they'd already murdered in Europe; the hundreds
killed in the battle of Berlin. It's no place for sentiment.
It was a bourgeois family murder, complete with

means, motive and opportunity. Do you really think that if it had been decided Helmut was to be the phoenix they would have worried?"

"Instinct tells me they wouldn't have accepted it. They were to die as a family. Magda and the children were offered protection. It was refused."

Cooling faltered, ready to launch into his examination of the children's deaths, when the red telephone buzzed.

Maitland-Wood spoke for a few seconds: monosyllables, terse and correct. When he replaced the instrument he looked preoccupied. "I have to see the Minister," he said. "Don't start on the paperwork until we've finished this conversation. Ideas are brewing, even though I detect a certain cynicism in your attitude."

Cooling forced a smile which came reluctantly to his lips. "I'm quite anxious to know who Werewolf is, and to find out if he's a threat or a dream. But there's only one way we'll know for sure."

"And what might that be?" He was already standing, a finger on the little panel of buttons by the bank of telephones; summoning some minion.

"You send in a pair of sympathetic confessors and let them sear his soul."

"We'll continue tomorrow morning at ten. Remember that both the Minister and myself are still beset by problems concerning agitators like Rivers, and nosey writers like Mr. Robin Chilton." The Deputy Director nodded: dismissive, too busy with affairs of state to bother with the end result of this evaluation. It's all part of a game, really, Cooling thought. This is merely a hobby. He wondered how seriously any of them took the true threats, the political burrowing, the anti-establishment unrest which could paralyse the country.

Back in his office, he shuffled the papers, looking for the last time at the way those six children had come to their end.

18

*The children are wonderful. They do everything
for themselves in these more than primitive surroundings. Whether or not they sleep on the floor
or get properly washed, or have enough to eat—
there is never a tear nor a word of complaint.
When gunfire shakes the bunker, the bigger ones
comfort the little ones. Their presence here is a
blessing, for they can always bring a smile to the
Führer's face.*

Cooling shook his head and put down the page:
Magda Goebbels' last letter from the bunker. He
flipped through the small series of documents in front
of him: the Soviet archive reports, the autopsy reports
and protocols of identification; the other pieces of evi-

dence: the photographs, the charred and grisly remains of Goebbels himself and his wife; the line of children's bodies in their night clothes, as though asleep; Helga Goebbels, dead and propped up in the arms of a spectacled Russian medical orderly, her lips swollen and cut but the young face at peace.

The fact that so many people told different stories was in itself an indication of the mystery. An unnamed woman claimed that Magda Goebbels, after participating in the murders, sobbed out her misery in one of the small rooms in the bunker. She had told them that they were going on a dream journey to Schwanenwerder—their much-loved home—but they were not deceived and she had dragged them screaming to the doctor for the fatal injections.

Others reported seeing her standing in the corridors, ashen-faced while a doctor, fingered variously as Hitler's surgeon, Stumpfegger, a Dr. Kunz, or Professor Haas, administered injections of Evipan or prussic acid.

Another story was that the poison was given, by Magda, in a spoon.

All the time Goebbels, himself, prepared for death by bringing his diary up to date. In the end his adjutant destroyed these last written pages, so the answer added up to a great zero.

The identification reports were bare, minimal. People, thought Cooling, had been identified on less. The five Goebbels girls were there in their night clothes—the boy, whichever boy, would naturally be taken to be

Helmut. Nobody was really going to think twice about it. Again he looked down the names of those who had identified the children and their parents: Vice-Admiral Voss, Karl Schneider, the Chancellery chief garage mechanic, and Wilhelm Lange, the Chancellery cook. *All knew Goebbels, his wife and children well,* it said.

Then the autopsy reports: Documents 1 to 11. Helga; Heide; Hedda; Holde; Helmut and Hilde. Each one had the same symptoms—splinters of ampule in mouth, brain matter smells of bitter almonds; chemical analysis, cyanides present; conclusion, cyanide poisoning.

Last, the Russian interrogation of Dr. Kunz, a dentist brought late in the bunker (April 23, 1945). There were two interrogations. In the first Kunz told of assisting Magda Goebbels, administering injections of morphine ("Children, don't be afraid, the doctor is going to give you an injection, a kind that is now given to all children and soldiers"). When they were asleep, he helped Magda crush the cyanide ampules into their mouths. That was his testimony on May 7, 1945. On May 19 he changed his tune. He gave them the injections but could not bring himself to assist in giving the poison. Dr. Stumpfegger had to be called for that. A small mystery.

Cooling saw that he had underlined one passage in the first interrogation of May 7. They were going to the children and Kunz stated: *As we left the study, that is, I and Frau Goebbels, two young persons in uniform,*

*'unknown to me, were sitting in the antechamber; one
wore the uniform of the Hitler Youth, I can't remember
how the other was dressed. Goebbels and his wife said
goodbye to the two.*

Was there significance? Who could tell? All Cooling
knew now was that the mystery of the last hours in
Berlin was deepened. He could go no further. If the
truth was really important they could only get it from
Gotterson: Werewolf. There was no more than that.

He rang Registry, and the clerk came to remove the
files. Tomorrow, he thought, there would be the final
interview with Maitland-Wood, then a couple of days'
work on the report. His job would be done. He was not
a trained confessor, adept in the techniques of reform
and cleaning the truth from damned souls.

There was still a half hour to kill before meeting
Steph, so he ran quickly through the latest wire reports
from Pine Copse End, which he would have to return
to Gibbs when he got back to the house. He had hardly
bothered with them this week. Werewolf talked to his
office queen bee. He was to go up north for a couple of
days (he would be there now). One of the Scandinavian Imports reps rang to arrange a London meeting: he thought he had found a new outlet—a big store
in Clapham. The whole conversation was loaded with
possible covert meanings—if you wanted to read them
that way. A clever lawyer could have twisted every
other word to make it look like the setting up of a neo-
Nazi rally. The ambiguity was staggering. Sybil Gotter-

son spoke with Cooling's mother; it was odd to read through that transcript, hearing his mother's voice coming from the typed dialogue ("Little Helen is so sweet. It's one of the things I long for—a grandchild. If only Vincent would get married."). Once more Werewolf spoke with Miss Anerson at his office. He wondered how much digging the DD had ordered on that front. If Werewolf was a far right wing, deep penetration political, then his links with the past might lead directly through Miss Anerson and Scandinavian Imports.

He locked the file in his briefcase, put on his coat and left the office. As he got into the lift, all the horrors fused together in his mind: the boy in the Hitler Youth uniform sitting against the cold and stark wall as Goebbels nodded to his wife and she went, with Kunz, towards the children's room to do what had to be done.

Joseph and Sybil Gotterson overlapped the image, dragging a screaming, tousled Helen towards a door, open and leading to the dark.

Once in the street, the weight lifted. He had virtually finished. Let the dead play their own tricks on the living; let them haunt Maitland-Wood and Gibbs, not him. Now was the time to live and Steph was waiting.

They had dinner in a small Italian place in Soho, relaxed, friendly, their conversation touching on the possibilities of the future.

"Will they send you back to Berlin?" she asked.

He did not know, but presumed he could wangle a

transfer; or was there any chance of her being sent back to Germany?

"I presume we have a future," her eyes grave, perhaps pleading.

"It's up to you, Steph. I personally don't subscribe to the idea that marriage is outdated. It just depends on what kind of marriage."

"You mean will I give up my career to have babies?"

"Something of the sort."

"You can't really have kids and let them fend for themselves." They had talked about it before: she would, in many ways, hate to give up her career and freedom, but marriage was always a compromise. "I love you," she said, simple and direct, without any clinging. "I'll resign if you want me to. Or try for a transfer."

In the end they decided to wait and see what his next posting would be.

"I shall know in a day or two. Does it have to be a big wedding?"

"I wouldn't want that, but the old folks at home," she shrugged, leaving it to his imagination.

They went back to Cheyne Walk in a taxi and he stayed until almost two in the morning.

Gibbs was waiting in the hall when he got in, his thin hair ruffled and a look of anxiety mixed into his pinched features.

"You're to call your mother straight away."

Greg came in behind him, through the front door as though he had been one of the shadows, a flickering look passing between him and Gibbs. Greg closed the front door and leaned on it.

"Use the study," Gibbs said, and for a second Cooling did not realise that he was speaking to him, telling him to use the house telephone. His hand shook as he dialled, as if his nervous system already knew of a pending disaster. The bell rang eight times before his mother answered. She started speaking almost straight away, and what she had to say turned his blood to ice.

19

Sybil had to fight the fear quite consciously. She tried
to be realistic, knowing that Joseph must get on with
his work. Yet she did not want to be left in the house
without him. It was inevitable, though, and she knew
that his patience would reach a low level of tolerance if
she nagged about it.

She calmed herself with the thought that at least
Marina would be there: and Helen. It was only for two
nights after all, and Joseph was not disturbed by the
house. He even joked about it so that she wondered if
it was her imagination; knowing that it was not, for
Marina had become more silent over the Christmas,
murmuring about the noises and crossing herself in the
hall before climbing the stairs. The carving knife which
had disappeared on the Sunday after Christmas had
not been found either, and that made Sybil anxious,

particularly when she remembered the business of the scissors.

On the morning Joseph left to go up north, she planned her time so that the whole two and a half days would be full—shopping in Farnham with Helen, little jobs which needed doing around the house. In the evenings there were the post-Christmas letters to be written. She might even ask the nice Mrs. Cooling over for the second evening.

Brownie was unhappy about his master's sudden desertion; and during the first day he whined about the house, whimpering at the study door.

"Brownie's silly, Mummy," little Helen said, watching the animal patting the door with his paws. "Daddy come home soon, Brownie. Be back soon."

That night they went to bed early. She took Brownie for his evening run and saw him into the utility room, which backed on to the kitchen. The dog seemed restless and she tried, again, to use reason. He was restless because Joseph was away. Uncertain, the animal settled in his basket but started whimpering as soon as she closed the door and tested the lock.

She made herself a milk drink (noticed that the sugar bowl was empty), saw Marina up the stairs, turned off the light and went to her room.

As soon as she got into bed, Sybil knew that she was not going to sleep. She plumped up the pillows at her back, sipped the drink, and tried to read one of her Christmas books. But neither plot nor characters held her mind. She skated over the words, skimming along the surface of the story without becoming involved. It was as if the largest part of her mind still roamed the house, peering into the dark corners downstairs, wandering along the landing to Helen's door. She might be a ghost herself, she thought, a mental projection of her own fears. Joseph could well be right about the whole thing being her imagination, for she could see into the dark places, like a camera lens tracking silently in the emptiness.

The first noise came just after midnight, distinct and clear, as though someone had switched on a record in Joseph's study. Far away, almost on the brink of her hearing, snatches of tiny sound. The goose-flesh rose on her arms, and at the roots of her hair she felt that cold, excruciating tingle. The sound (a voice?), then silence. Again, then gone, leaving what seemed to be an echo in her head. A small voice, heard at a great distance, borne on the air, singing, a minute fragment of a song, the resultant silence louder than the sound.

She tried to read, but it was there, behind the words, far away, yet close, as near to her as the landing. Then Brownie began to call in a high, excited whine: not a bark of warning but a shriek of fear, continuous and loud, followed by a very real crash and footsteps—pattering, distant yet there, below in the hall and on the stairs: and now a scrape on her door, close, loud and quite distinct.

In spite of her terror, for the whole house seemed to

be roused, Sybil threw back the bedclothes, grabbed at her housecoat and leaped for the door, tugging it open, and not knowing what to expect.

As she reached the landing, all the other noises subsided, leaving the dog's melancholy wail a lonely solo. Then Marina appeared from the corridor, sheet white, eyes staring.

"What with the dog?" She repeated three or four times, "The dog. The dog," crossing herself.

Sybil took a deep breath and put on the hall light from the landing switch. Brownie's whimper did not stop; it went on like a child frightened in the dark, a baying, almost human, sobbing.

"See if Helen's all right," Sybil said, amazed at her voice and the calmness of it. Marina retreated down the passage, and as she did so, Sybil heard, from behind her, the tapping against the bedroom window, as though a bird was seeking entrance, disoriented and without the sense to turn away. She had seen small birds in daylight fluttering against the glass, confused by their reflection. But this was night and the sound was persistent.

"She sleeps." Marina returned, red dressing gown around her shoulders, open so that Sybil could see her body clearly through the opaque nightdress underneath.

"We'll have to go and see to the dog," Sybil's voice still firm, belying the thud of her heart and the breathlessness in her throat.

She went to the top of the stairs, pausing to beckon to Marina, then plunged downwards, almost running, like one who is nervous of diving into a swimming pool yet determined to get the unpleasantness over quickly, refusing the gentle descent into the cold.

She ran down the hall, her hand fumbling for the door and then the kitchen light, stopping suddenly, clinging to the door jamb with a gasp at the sight before her.

The door at the far end of the kitchen was still closed tight, from behind it Brownie's cry continued, as though in pain and fear. Between the kitchen and utility-room doors there was turmoil.

The sugar bowl lay shattered in the centre of the floor, and the store cupboard door hung open, tins and packets cascading out as if pulled from the shelves by someone engaged in a frenzied search. Two packets of sugar had been almost ripped apart, their contents scattered across the floor. The windows were closed and there was no sign of whatever had done this senseless vandalism.

She picked her way through the mess—Marina left by the door, muttering prayers—and tested the door to the utility room. It was still fast. She turned the knob and threw it open, the kitchen light spreading across the stone floor in a great rectangle, revealing the dog, shivering and cowed, in the corner.

For a second the animal hesitated, then, with a frightened yelp, he ran forward, brushing past her. She had the impression that its hair was literally raised on end, and it moved as though something horrible was after it.

By that time Sybil had the utility-room light on and could plainly see that there was nothing out of place. She turned back to Marina.

"I not stay. I not stay here. Evil. Bad." The girl's head moved from side to side as though she was on the brink of a fit, and as Sybil retraced her steps over the crunching sugar, they both heard the screams from upstairs.

"Helen," Sybil heard herself shout loud above the child's shrieks, but she could still distinguish the words, run together and possibly inaudible to all but a mother.

"Don't let it, Mummy. The baby, don't let it. Don't let it."

She grabbed at the skirt of her housecoat and ran back down through the hall, shouting to Helen that it was all right, that Mummy was here. She could hear the child running above her, reaching the landing as she got to the middle of hall. Then, a moment of distraction as she felt some object coming down through the stairwell. It caught her on the shoulder and bounced down with a ringing metal clatter onto the bare boards.

She glanced towards the object and saw it was the carving knife, then upwards, shouting out as the hysterical child got to the top of the stairs, tottered and fell, bouncing like a doll from the top to bottom.

20

"She's quite calm now, in the spare bedroom; and little Helen's already asleep." Cooling's mother spoke quietly into his ear. "It's only the wretched foreign girl who's any trouble: sitting in the kitchen, crying and saying prayers; playing with her rosary."

She went over the bare facts, just as Sybil had poured them out to her when she had arrived, pounding on the door of the flat.

"You're sure the child's not hurt?" he asked.

"Got a bruise the size of an egg on her forehead, but she'll be fine. Children of that age often fall downstairs. You did. Twice. You only worry if there's silence when they reach the bottom. Young Helen bawled her head off. Must've wakened the whole of Scholars Road. I thought you should know immediately. Because of your interest."

"Thank you. Yes."

"I suppose we'd better ring Mr. Gotterson in the morning."

"I expect so." He cursed the fact that he was on the house phone. Somewhere, a tape was taking it all down. "Don't do anything until I get in touch."

"I'll be sleeping in here, beside the phone. You can ring any time you like."

"I'll be on as soon as possible. She can't hear?"

"No. Maybe she's asleep by now."

"You believe it all, Mother?"

A pause before she answered. He could see her, peeling a cigarette from her lips, sitting there on a chair arm.

"She's had a shock. A fright. I think she's got an active imagination as well. Maybe she's on the right wavelength for these things. Who knows? The business in the kitchen? I suspect that damned Alsatian."

"Keep her there, anyway. I'll be in touch."

He closed the line and sat still, thinking for a few moments. When he went through to the hall Maitland-Wood stood by the drawing-room door with Gibbs.

"What happened?" The Deputy Director still had his coat on: black, waisted, double-breasted with a little velvet collar. Cooling thought they probably considered him a dandy at the Ministry.

"Don't you know?" Cooling wanted to shout. "Don't you really know? What godless games have you been playing in that house?"

Maitland-Wood made a gesture, both arms, a sign of hopelessness.

Gibbs looked at him with dead eyes. "We've got the phone wired, and there're a couple of sneakies in the house. That's all. They picked up the dog and the women: the crash. Then the screams—the child. Our eavesdropper thought it was an intruder."

For half a minute they stood facing each other, a triangle in the hall. Then the Deputy Director motioned them into the drawing room. As Gibbs stood back to let Cooling follow Maitland-Wood, Greg appeared from the stairs, handing him some sheets of typescript.

"You swear to me that you haven't been playing tricks on them?" Cooling stood, refusing the proffered chair.

"You're in no position to ask me to swear to anything." Maitland-Wood reached towards the decanters, then changed his mind, scanning the typescript which Gibbs handed to him. It was Cooling's conversation with his mother.

"Hysteria?" asked Gibbs, eyebrows arching.

The Deputy Director did not answer. He was looking at Cooling.

"What do you believe about this sort of thing?"

"What? The haunted house? Pine Copse End?"

"That in particular. The paranormal in general."

"Ghosties and ghoulies? Tonight could be a culmination of a lot of things. She was very nervous about the place when I met her at Christmas. The nervousness could be transferred to the child, the dog even. I'd lay odds on the dog doing the damage in the kitchen."

"The paranormal?" repeated Maitland-Wood.

"Open mind. All *in* the mind. Projections. Maybe I believe in the imprint theory, past and present hanging around to be picked up by someone on the right nervous wavelength."

"You really believe all that?" Surprised, a little shocked even.

"There is evidence. I also believe in poltergeist phenomena."

The Deputy Director nodded. "The house does have a history." He seemed to be speaking to himself. "How best can we turn it to our own advantage?"

"Werewolf isn't impressed by any of it." Gibbs stifled a yawn.

Maitland-Wood smiled. "Then he'll have to be tuned to the right station." His eyes switched, slowly, to Cooling. "How convincing could you be about matters psychical?"

"I know the words—psychokinesis, telekinesis, psychometry, cold spots. The jargon."

"He means he's read the right books," Gibbs sighed.

"People down there, in Tilt, think you're a researcher?"

"That's what my mother tells them. Mainly industrial research."

"How about breaking the news to them that your particular forte is psychic research?"

"To what end?"

"Getting the Gottersons out. Just for a weekend. So you can do a few tests."

"You'd need to test the personalities to be convincing."

Maitland-Wood nodded again, eyelids drooping. "Yes, but the house first. One week-end with *carte blanche.*"

"For what?"

"Nothing much. Just so we can have a look-see."

"I don't know if he'd wear it. She gave me the impression that he's sceptical."

"Have a go?"

"Is there a choice?"

"Not really."

Maitland-Wood pulled himself out of the chair. "Ring your mother again, break the news. Greg and Bud'll take you down. I want the Gottersons out for the week-end."

"And if they won't go?"

"Then we'll have to think of something else. Come straight back to Tony. As secure as you can make it."

Gibbs was moving like a warder, pressing him towards the door. Cooling remembered Scandinavian Imports.

"You checked his business?"

"The furniture store?" The Deputy Director buttoned his coat. "One of the first things we did. It's clean. The whole thing's genuine: or very careful cover. Everyone comes out pure and sanitized, right back to their conceptions."

"So they're either playing it very long with a lot of help, or it is for real?"

"And Werewolf's on his own. Please go and call your mother. Tell her we'll try not to be any bother."

They did not get down to Tilt until just after seven in the morning. Cooling rang his mother, giving her the brief facts, wishing he could say more. He threw things into a case and wrote a swift note to Steph—saying his mother was not well and he might be away for a couple of days. In all he was ready by half-past three. But, as usual, there were hold-ups, and the car did not arrive until almost five-thirty. After that there were some technical problems.

He dozed all the way down, and they dropped him, in the early morning gloom, at the bottom of Scholars Road. His mother greeted him with the news that Marina had left. The Portuguese girl had summoned all her courage, backed by the prayers of Holy Church, and gone across the road to Pine Copse End, dressed, crammed her belongings into two suitcases and caught the first bus into Farnham, muttering that she could never sleep under that roof again.

"Is the house still open?" He sipped coffee from a mug in the chill, but very normal, atmosphere of his mother's living room.

"I gather the front door was left open when they ran

over here." She had obviously chain smoked through the night, for the ashtray was piled with stubbed butts and ash. "I presume that stupid girl didn't shut it. Why?"

"I thought I might walk over and take a look. What do you make of it, Mum?"

She blinked. It occurred to him that his mother often looked like a wise old owl. An attractive owl.

"I really don't know, dear. The mother and child were hysterical. The girl was merely superstitious. Wouldn't surprise me if she attracted things like this."

Cooling put the thought away, filing it for future use. "And they're still asleep?"

"Like babes, both of them."

"I'll go and take a walk around the place. Keep your fingers crossed that it's not a daylight ghost."

"What's it really all about, son?"

"Three wise monkeys. Better that way. My boss said we'd try not to bother you over much."

"It's no bother. Nice to have a bit of excitement once in a while."

Brownie greeted him at the door, suspicious with a deep growl. He offered the Alsatian the back of his hand and talked gently. After all, it was still only a puppy. The animal showed no sign of fear, now, and followed him into the house.

The lights still burned and, on the bare boards in the middle of the hall, the carving knife glinted, its point towards the door.

When they got to the kitchen, Brownie held back
and began to whimper.

"You're a bad lad," Cooling chided softly. "A right
tearaway."

There were scratches on the store cupboard door,
which had a small metal trim around it. The dog could
have got it open with ease: it sniffed around now at his
feet, among the scattered tins, making little whining
sounds.

Towards the back of the cupboard, Cooling saw a
bag of dog biscuits, one side torn open. There were also
some tins of dog food. He took one out and looked
around for a tin opener, finding it attached to the Ken-
wood Chef which stood on the working surface near
the sink.

The dog's feeding bowls were through in the utility
room, and when he brought them into the kitchen, he
found Brownie happily licking up the spilled sugar
from the floor.

"Yes, you like that, don't you?"

He filled the bowls, one with water, the other with
the contents of the tin, then took them through to the
utility room, calling the dog, who came trotting after
him.

His feet crunched on the sugar as he turned back
into the kitchen, looking from the utility-room door to
the one which gave access to the kitchen. Sybil Gotterson had closed the utility-room door on Brownie before

going to bed. It had still been closed when she reached the vandalised kitchen.

Cooling pulled the utility door shut, holding the knob and testing the catch. It remained firm. Then he took his hand from the knob and pressed against the wood. The catch slipped and the door swung open. The tongue on the lock was worn bright, smooth and shiny.

Pulling the door closed again, he picked his way over the debris to the kitchen door, which he shut firmly, pulling it well back before slamming it forward. As the door clicked into place he felt the draught over the tiled floor and saw the utility door slip its catch and swing outwards. Brownie could have got back into the kitchen.

If it worked in reverse, then one of the mysteries could be solved. Reaching down, Cooling pulled the kitchen door sharply open. Across the room the utility door seemed to be sucked to by the draught. He even heard the worn tongue click into place. So much for Brownie being locked in, he smiled.

The rest of the house appeared clean, and the only room he could not enter was the study. The door from the drawing room was firmly locked. He did not disturb anything or open the drawers or cupboards. That could be left to Tony Gibbs and his merry men. He did not particularly like the idea of persuading the Gottersons to leave so that the house could be probed, but, as Maitland-Wood had said, there was no alternative. It could prove to be the more painless way.

When he got back to his mother's flat, Helen was sitting on several cushions in an armchair, drinking a beaker of milk, watched over by Mrs. Cooling.

"Hallo, you're Helen."

"Yes," her eyes wide. "What's your name?"

"That's my little boy," began his mother.

"Once upon a time I was her little boy. My name's Vincent."

"Helen's being nice and quiet in here while her Mummy gets some more sleep."

"Good." He smiled at Helen, who beamed back. His mother was giving him questioning looks.

"You had a bit of a bad dream last night, then, Helen?"

"Mmmm," she shook her head violently. "I slept in a bed with Mummy and I came to tea the other day."

"I know. What was your dream about?"

"Can't remember. Don't know."

"Was there a baby in the dream?"

"There's a baby in the house that cries and wakes me up. Naughty Brownie cried and wake me up in the night."

"Yes, and you fell downstairs."

"Got a bruise." She lifted a hand to her head where the skin showed blue, turning to black. The suggestion brought tears to her eyes and her lip began to quiver.

"There, it's all right now, Helen. Remember, we put some butter on it last night," his mother cooed, massaging the lump with her hand.

"I want Mummy," the descent into tears imminent.

"See what you've done now," his mother mouthed.

"Mummy, Mummy, Mummy," wailed the child.

Mrs. Cooling rescued the beaker of milk and began to hug Helen, rocking her in her arms and making calming noises.

"Come on, we don't want to wake Mummy yet, do we?"

"It's okay, Mummy's awake." Sybil stood in the doorway. She had a marked, thin, drawn and pinched look. Then she saw Cooling. "Oh, I didn't realise you were . . ."

"How are you after all the excitement?" Vincent smiled, rising and offering his hand.

"Oh . . ." A little embarrassed. "Have you just arrived or what?"

"I was coming down anyway. My mother rang me during the night. She thought I might be able to help."

"Help?"

"Mummy, I had a dream about the baby again. Mummy."

Helen began to struggle away from Mrs. Cooling, making a dive towards Sybil.

"Yes, darling, now hush a minute."

"And I've got a lump. We rubbed butter on it. Naughty Brownie woke us all up."

"You come with me, Helen. We'll get Mummy and Vincent a nice cup of coffee." Mrs. Cooling grasped her by the hand.

The child began to whine and pull away.

"Go on, darling. Go and help Mrs. Cooling."

Reluctantly, Helen followed the older woman to the kitchen, looking back over her shoulder, dragging her feet.

"Help?" repeated Sybil.

"I shall have to come clean." He removed the cushions on which Helen had been sitting and indicated the chair. "My mother tells most people that I do industrial research. I keep up the fiction for her sake. I think she feels the village might think me rather strange. I am in research. Psychic research. So she thought I might help."

The sound of singing came from the kitchen: Mrs. Cooling's English Hymnal voice blending with a tuneless warble from the child.

> "Georgie Porgie pudding and pie,
> Kissed the girls and made them cry;
> When the boys came out to play . . ."

"He kissed them too, he's funny that way," murmured Cooling.

Sybil grinned.

"That's better. You want to tell me about it?"

She went over the whole story again. It was pretty much as his mother had told him on the telephone.

"Am I going mad?" she asked.

"Not at all. There are stories about the house. You're

nervous in it at night. It seems a very normal reaction to me."

"It's not just me. Marina's terrified. Where is she, by the way? She should be looking after Helen."

Cooling told her.

"Oh, Christ: she was so good." She looked even more weary at the thought of having to cope on her own.

"It may be a blessing in disguise. If you want me to get a team together and examine the house, I will. I also think we should do some experiments on the people concerned: you, Helen and, if possible, Marina."

"Experiments?"

"Simple tests. I hope you don't mind, but I've been over there already. I'm sure you believe that you heard things, and I think there might just be a basis for that belief. Some people are attuned to hearing, and seeing things. You may be one. Marina might be as well. Or she could be sparking off poltergeist phenomena. By the way, I think the dog did most of it."

"But he was . . ."

"Shut up in the room off the kitchen? Yes, I know. If we can go back to the house, I'll show you what I think happened."

An hour later, they had Helen safely playing in the nursery and Cooling demonstrated how the utility-room door could have been open and then came to be closed when Sybil had rushed into the kitchen.

"But I've heard the noises before. Before Brownie ever came into the house." She told him about the sugar and the little footsteps, the scissors and the carving knife. "Last night there was someone singing. A child."

"Definitely a child, or only a child because you know the story about the house?"

"You don't believe me."

He tried to be calm and patient, convincing, pushing away the ever-present thought that he was talking to Werewolf's wife.

"I believe that some strange things have happened to you here—and to the child. It's most probable that there are very strong memories locked away here. You might be picking them up like a radio."

"What can I do? I can't stay here alone for another night."

"If it could be explained to you: rationally, scientifically, it might put your mind at rest. You could come to terms with it."

"I don't know. What're you suggesting?"

"I'd like to bring some colleagues down here—just for a couple of days. We'd make tests with instruments: changes of temperature, measuring draughts, recordings even. Some of the things you've heard might be explained. Later we would do tests with you and Helen back in the house."

"You can't explain the scissors and the carving knife?"

"Not yet, but . . ."

"You'd like to stay here alone? Without anyone else?"

"That would be best."

"Joseph comes back tomorrow. How much time would you need?"

"Oh, two or three nights. Look, it's Thursday now; perhaps until Sunday night, or Monday morning."

"I don't know. He's not very tolerant about my being nervous. He says I'm imagining things."

"If I talked to him?"

"Would you?"

They tracked Joseph Gotterson down at the Piccadilly Hotel in Manchester. At first he was anxious about his wife, then slightly impatient and suspicious.

"You mean to tell me you actually do scientific research into things like this?"

"I'm absolutely serious, Mr. Gotterson. I'm not a crank."

"No, you seemed perfectly normal when we met, but it is so fantastic."

"Mrs. Gotterson was very frightened. And Helen," he lowered his voice. "Often, in these cases there are simple explanations. It would dispel her fear of the place if we could assure her that . . ."

"You wish to stay in my house on your own?"

"With a few colleagues. My mother would be here as well. I do think it might help your wife, and I can promise that we'll do no damage."

"Well, I suppose . . ." He was not convinced. "Let me talk to Sybil."

Cooling listened to one side of the conversation, which started off in a stilted fashion, then gradually relaxed. Within five minutes he knew he had won.

"I've to ring the office and get Miss Anerson to make arrangements. We're all going to stay in some nice hotel that Joseph knows in the north." She was more herself now. "He says that you can stay here, but you cannot use his study. If tests have to be made there, you'll have to do them when we get back on Monday."

Cooling went over to the flat while Sybil rang Scandinavian Imports and made the other arrangements.

"I think they'll be out by this afternoon," he told Gibbs on the telephone to the house near St. James's.

"Let me know as soon as she gives you a time." He sounded businesslike, very operational, closing the line almost before the conversation was finished.

Sybil and Helen left in a taxi at three o'clock. Miss Anerson would meet them at Waterloo and take them on.

"I expect Joseph will ring you at the house. Oh, and I've put towels out, and there are three beds made up. You'll see to Brownie, won't you?"

Cooling promised to look after the dog, then he went inside and phoned Gibbs again. Less than ten minutes later a car pulled up in the drive.

"I've been hanging around in Farnham for almost two hours," said Maitland-Wood. He had a small man with him, shifty-eyed and quick in his movements. "Gibbs'll be here with the team after dark. There's a lot to be done."

"The study's locked. He says we can't use it."

"Cromer'll fix that." The Deputy Director nodded towards the little man. "Cromer's a locksmith."

They went into the hall, their shoes sounding like a dozen men on the bare boards.

"We can have the place combed out in an evening." Cooling patted the Alsatian, who was making up his mind about them—a little confused.

"I dare say." Maitland-Wood took his coat off, folding it neatly as he crossed into the drawing room. "Is that a real Lowry?"

"I think it is." Cromer's voice matched his build. "Yes, it looks like the real McCoy. That the door?"

Cooling told him that it was, and Cromer crossed to the study door and began rattling the knob.

"Returning on Monday, you say?" The Deputy Director went on examining the painting. "Yes, it's very nice. Good hedge, Lowry. Good appreciation."

"Monday morning."

"Just enough time, then."

"For what?" Cooling felt an involuntary shudder.

"You want to know who he is, don't you? I want to know who he is; and the Minister wants him out." He smiled, bland and conspiratorial. "You don't think we're going to do all that with a search, do you? No,

Vincent, you're going to mount an operation: you're going into the ghost business. You're going to freak him. Amusing, isn't it? Especially when one considers that we in the trade are often known as spooks."

21

Cooling stood his ground. "What d'you mean we're going to freak him? Get into the ghost business?"

"I said *you* were going to get into the ghost business," the smile trickling from Maitland-Wood's lips like thin gravy. "It's quite simple. Some sophisticated *son et lumière;* sneakies and peeps. A line into his television so we can feed him a few subliminals; whisper in his ear. It'll be quite safe. You'll have a psychiatrist watching him."

"What are you talking about, feeding him subliminals and whispering in his ear?"

"Get his mind going on the past. Take him back to the bunker and Uncle Adolf—if he is Helmut, that's what he called him, you know? Uncle Adolf, or Uncle Führer."

"For Christ's sake," his voice rising above its normal

apogee. "There'll be a woman and child here. You'll be putting them at the other end of it as well."

Out of the corner of his eye he saw Cromer kneel down by the study door and take out a small canvas wallet. He unrolled it on the carpet, displaying a series of metal instruments: probes and things like dental instruments. If Cromer was a genuine locksmith, Cooling thought, he was Steve McQueen.

"And you want me to carry the can?" He felt physically sick. "If something goes wrong . . . ?"

"It'll look better on paper." Maitland-Wood turned away, gazing at Cromer and his lock-picking with studied interest.

"I'm damned if I will," he spoke quietly but with enough conviction to turn the Deputy Director's head towards him.

"You'll be damned if you don't." Maitland-Wood flicked his eyes in the direction of the door: an order.

"You're earmarked for this one," he said once they were in the hall, "and you'll do as you're told."

"Or you'll give me a dose of the measles? Death from natural causes and a hero's grave?"

Maitland-Wood did not smile. "Oh no," it was almost matter-of-fact. "Much more unpleasant. Miss Stephanie Bishop gets her name wrapped around an international sex scandal. Call girl in her spare time, all that kind of thing. Did I ever show you the Maubert photographs?"

Cooling had known it all along: the three-way split:

a triple satisfaction. They probably would not even have leaned on Steph in the normal course of events. When the opportunity presented itself, though, the Deputy Director must have seen it as a chance to keep him in order—should the need arise. Now it had arisen.

He saw Steph in the half light of his mind, straining naked on a bed, her partner not distinct enough to be recognised. He'd be identifiable in the photographs, though. The image was immediately overlapped by the recurring picture of the soldier and the boy among the rubble.

"It's not a nice thought." Maitland-Wood stepped closer and Cooling caught the smokey odor of cigar and expensive after shave. "But don't for a moment think that we would not resort to that kind of violence. Come on, Vincent. This operation'll be good for your soul."

"It's open," Cromer called from the drawing room, and they went back inside to examine Joseph Gotterson's study.

"I don't particularly want to stay here for too long." Maitland-Wood balanced himself on a stiff upright chair as they sorted through the correspondence from the drawers in Gotterson's desk. "There's too much to do in town. But Gibbs and his team'll be here in no time. I've spoken to your mother, by the way, Vincent; on the telephone. She has no objection to our using her place as a command post. She'd have been good in the trade, your mother."

She had said that she would not mind a little excitement. "Do we have to use her flat?" Cooling asked.

"I think so. It's very handy. There's nowhere else really."

"You've had a wire on the telephone here since the Gottersons moved in," Cooling trying to spin it out; reclaim the initiative in a game already lost. "Where's your eavesdropper been hiding himself?"

"He's a rover. Got a nice little van with a bed in the back. He tucks it away all over the place." He continued to scrutinise the pile of business letters. "I'll say one thing for Gotterson's cover—if it is cover—meticulous. All the figures look good, and all this bumph. Dear sir, regarding yours. All done properly."

"You said yourself that his business is whiter than white."

"Pine Copse End, Tilt, Near Farnham, Surrey," Maitland-Wood muttered to himself. "Wonder why he chose here? Tilt? Be the end of him, Vincent. You ever play pinball?"

"Not really."

"Fascinating. The kids have got a machine in their music room. Music? Cacophony. Tilt. You know what happens if you tilt a pinball machine while you're in play, Vincent?"

Cooling shook his head.

"Lose your balls, old son. Lose your balls."

Cromer guffawed. He was working on the one desk drawer that was locked.

"You losing your balls, Cromer?" Jaunty: the public school prefect to his fag. It was the kind of humour that Maitland-Wood must've excelled at in school (*Cut along, Cromer, or you'll lose your balls, you cretinous tick*).

Cromer guffawed again. He had a subservient humour, Cooling decided: one who laughed at jokes made by his seniors no matter what the wit.

"Got it," said Cromer, and they heard the drawer slide back. "Treasure trove here, sir."

They went around to the other side of the desk. In the shallow drawer lay half a dozen objects. A Mauser automatic pistol and two magazines, both loaded; an SS long-service medal with the runic lightning flashes on one side; an Iron Cross first class and a small enamel and gold Nazi Party badge.

"Clincher." The Deputy Director held the Iron Cross in the palm of his hand as though testing its weight. "Convinced now, Vincent?"

"I've always been convinced that he came out of Germany. I just don't think there's much of a case against him on any other count. Or are you old school, sir? The only good German is . . ."

Maitland-Wood tossed the medal back into the drawer. "We'll see." He snapped the drawer shut and told Cromer to lock it again. As if he was closing a file forever.

Gibbs and the team arrived just after six. A car and two vans, the second of which declared that it came from the Post Office. Maitland-Wood made hurried farewells and took Gibbs over to see Cooling's mother.

"We'll get the stuff into Mrs. Cooling's flat during the hours of darkness," Gibbs said when he came back. Then, as if an afterthought, "If that's okay by you?"

"Why shouldn't it be?"

"You are in charge of all this." When Gibbs swallowed, his Adam's apple jerked up and down.

"Only on paper. You do what you want."

Gibbs nodded and started giving orders. Around seven, just as they were breaking for coffee and sandwiches which they had brought from London, Joseph Gotterson telephoned.

"Are your people there with you?" he asked.

"Yes, they're all here. Setting up the equipment." Cooling wondered where Sybil was, and the child.

"What kind of equipment?"

"I've told Mrs. Gotterson. Just for measuring temperatures and for recording. We have some cameras as well, but we don't expect any joy from those."

"As long as everything is all right."

"Perfectly, Mr. Gotterson. I promise you, this'll set Mrs. Gotterson's mind at rest."

"You have my number in case anyone . . . ?"

"We'll telephone if there's any need."

He went back into the Gottersons' drawing room, where everybody had settled down and made themselves comfortable. One of the men from the Post

Office van even went off to the pub to get some bottled beer. They were electricians, Gibbs told him. Later, Vincent excused himself and walked up to the village to phone Steph from the local call box.

"How is she?" Steph asked straight away. He had to think for a few seconds in order to get back inside his cover and realise that she was talking about his mother, who he had said was ill.

"Sleeping. That's why I've come out to phone."

"You want me to come down and give you a hand?"

He had dreaded the possibility of the question, and eventually parried it by saying that his mother would only fuss with someone else in the flat.

"I should be back in a day or two," lying, for it could take weeks and he knew it.

"Sooner the better."

It was an uncomfortable conversation. He never felt happy about telephones at the best of times, bred as he was to consider them insecure methods of communication. Great gaps of things left unsaid yawned between them.

"It's all right, isn't it?" she asked towards the end.

"What?"

"Us, you fool. I'm sorry, that must sound awful."

"We're fine. We'll sort out things as soon as I'm back in London."

"No joy about your posting yet?"

"I'm working on it. You'll see."

He trudged back down Cricket Lane and into Scholars Road in the dark, noticing that there was a light in his mother's window.

The two electricians had a manhole up near the gates of Pine Copse End and were working, under emergency lights, with all the simulated Post Office gear around them.

Apart from these two, Gibbs had brought down a pair of wiremen and a couple of labourers.

Through the existing telephone and electricity system they ran a pair of land lines into Heath Corner and his mother's flat; the rest of the stuff was all radio VHF and already the house looked a mess.

Son et lumière, the Deputy Director had said. *Peeps and sneakies*. The peeps were closed-circuit television cameras, remote-controlled and dug into the walls. When the plaster and brick were made good again, and dirtied to its original finish, the pin lenses surveyed rooms through holes no bigger than a pencil end. They had one in the drawing room, another in the study, the third mounted on the outside wall of the kitchen, fourth and fifth in the hall and at the top of the staircase. The last, Cooling was disturbed to see, viewed the bedroom. He taxed Gibbs about it; but he only shrugged.

"Nobody's bothered about erotica," he said stiffly. "It's all part of the job."

Cooling should have known better. Gibbs and all like him were puritanical and held their own moral courts martial over the lives of others. They could look at other people's private follies without being tainted.

The sneakies had been laid out all over the house, ready for insertion. By the following evening they were all in place, the walls back to normal, teased into their rightful shades and textures by the labourers, so that by Saturday morning the house was, as Gibbs put it, wired for the spectacular.

There remained one or two more sophisticated bits of business such as locking into the television set by way of one of the land lines, fitting the existing loudspeakers—both television and Joseph's stereo—with special receivers and amplifiers, and several miniature high-frequency amplifiers inserted into walls at a safe distance from the sneakies. Six transducers were also set in place—the study, drawing room, kitchen, hall, landing and bedroom. When activated they would bounce back normal sounds with immense magnification, making a whisper into an echoed shout.

In the early hours of Sunday morning they moved the monitoring screens, the video machines, recorders and transmitters into Mrs. Cooling's living room.

Cooling was surprised that she was taking it so calmly.

"Your nice Mr. Maitland-Wood asked if I would mind you tramping about for a few days," she said, grinning in an almost conspiratorial way. "I've promised to stay out of the living room and I'll keep you all supplied with hot tea. It's getting to look like something from *Mission Impossible* in there." She poked her head nosily around the door.

Mission Improbable, Cooling thought: he had already had one brush with Gibbs that day.

"We laughed at the CIA with their wild schemes against Castro," he had snapped, "now we're following in their costly footsteps. Why don't you just proclaim the second coming of Hitler from the lawn and see how Gotterson reacts."

Throughout Sunday they tested and adjusted the entire system. Every word spoken in the house could be heard through the receivers in the flat, while the monitor screens gave off their eerie grey views, slightly distorted and blurred at the edges.

They also checked their playback systems and Cooling considered that he was never likely to forget standing in the drawing room, and later in Joseph's study, hearing a soft whisper emanating from the walls or from the middle of the room.

The link with the television set needed no adjustment: the normal programmes could be cut into without any trouble, sharply and with no loss of quality. By Sunday afternoon Joseph's study door was locked again and the house bore no trace of its visitors. During the whole time nobody had been disturbed by creaking boards, strange voices of crying babies, and the only thing that appeared in any way affected was the dog, Brownie, who had been so nervous that they had kept him in the utility room for the bulk of the week-end.

Only Cooling bothered to take him out for his runs across the recreation ground.

On Sunday evening the vans drove away, leaving only Tony Gibbs, the two wiremen—Watts and Cheesman—with Cooling. Around nine o'clock the psychiatrist arrived, accompanied by a technician who carried two metal fireproof cases filled with numbered cassettes and video tapes.

The psychiatrist reminded Cooling of photographs of Himmler. He was not like him at all, so Cooling supposed it was the wire-framed spectacles that did it. He was a man of unidentifiable age with white hair which looked out of place with his face. They were to call him Harvester, he said, though whether this was his real name or one of the Deputy Director's cryptonyms, Cooling could not decide. He was deferential to Cooling and made it plain that he was merely at their disposal for advice—"If things aren't moving as fast as you would like or if the subject is getting a shade frayed around the edges." His voice had a patient edge to it and Cooling guessed that he doubled as a confessor.

On Gibbs' suggestion, they ran a watch through the Sunday night on a rota basis of two on and two off, with Harvester and the technician on standby.

At about three o'clock in the morning, Cooling was monitoring the sound, room by room through earphones, when he thought he could pick up some alien noise. Watts, who shared his watch, heard nothing, but Cooling could have sworn that somewhere in the vicinity of the stairs he could hear a tiny noise: not quite human. Far away, almost a distant singing, tuneless and unstable. In the end he presumed that it was either a tiny draught of air or some freak feedback from the high-frequency signal transmitters. The screens showed nothing, only the darkness of the rooms, which seemed to be waiting for their occupants to invest them with life.

The Gottersons arrived back at a little after noon on the Monday.

Book Three:

SPECTRES YET TO COME

22

The reason for this particular memory was transparently obvious. A June afternoon—it must have been in 1950 or '51. There were two other boys with Cooling, one called Osterby; the other, a plump lad with glasses, he could not name. They had lain in the long fresh grass, prone and silent, watching and waiting for the couple to come slowly, hand in hand, up the rise to settle comfortably in the shelter of a clump of low bushes.

Osterby said that they always went there on a Sunday afternoon. He was a lover of wild life and had inadvertently been the unseen watcher of this human rising sap ritual three times already. From the long grass they had an unrestricted view of the couple, who were obviously only concerned about being seen from the road below.

At a distance of so many years, Cooling only remembered small details. In his mind there was no absolute picture of the pair of coupling bodies, nor even their faces. He saw only the man's white shirt, the girl's mouth, wide and gaping, slashed by smudged lipstick, the perfection of the grass spear scratching at his face, the scent of it and the sense that they were adhering to some rubric, going through automatic moves, like a game.

This act of teen-age voyeurism in no way excited him, rather he was sickened by it and had felt a strange guilt ever since. It was odd, for the guilt always returned when he watched love scenes in the cinema. It was a guilt which he supposed might have intruded into his daily work in Berlin, for that was a kind of voyeurism also; yet his conscience did not seem to prick him on that score. Only now, seated in the drawing-room of Pine Copse End, spilling out his fictional catalogue of the week-end ghost hunt, acutely aware of the hidden pin lenses and the multitude of listening devices, did Cooling feel uncomfortable.

He wanted to turn on Joseph, warn him and plead—for God's sake, whoever you were in that other world, that other life, bring it out into the open now: tell us who and why, and save everyone from the horrors which might come.

"So, what you are telling us is that you think all this is in my wife's mind?" Joseph asked as Cooling completed his solo performance.

"I don't think it is as simple as that." He was aware that much of what he had said was unconvincing, insubstantial, and he wondered what Gibbs and Harvester, locked into the screens and headphones, would be thinking.

On the carpet before the big bow window little Helen played quietly, absorbed in a pile of coloured plastic hollow bricks.

"It sounds as though I'm ready for a head doctor." Sybil's hand played with the saucer of her teacup, a finger tracking around the rim.

"Not at all." Cooling smiled, attempting to put her at ease. "I've already said that some people have the ability to pick up memories, to act like radio receivers on past events. You are very much aware of an appalling tragedy which happened here. Maybe some of it remains. Perhaps you are the recipient of the strong traces. That's not very scientific, I know, but it is one answer, and that's why we have to do some tests with you."

"When?"

"Soon. A week or so. In the meantime I'd like you to make notes of anything that happens to you . . ."

"Any strange vibrations? The sounds and voices?"

He nodded. "There's nothing to be afraid of." He was conscious of the lie. "There's nothing to harm you. You must be sure of that."

"I'll try to remember," a small nervous laugh; then they all turned as Brownie scratched at the door.

Joseph went over to let the Alsatian in, patting him and fussing, though with a firmness in his voice as he ordered the animal to sit.

"He has got a little disoriented with all this. I'm going to have to spend a lot of time with him."

"I tried to keep him away from the rest of my team while we were here," Cooling told him, knowing it was a lame remark.

When Joseph took him to the door, Cooling did his best to maintain the sense of unconcern.

"I find all this talk of the paranormal very strange," the hint of suspicion had slunk into Joseph's icy eyes. "It is something which I neither like, believe nor understand."

"D'you mean that you can't see why people examine it?"

"I see nothing at all. Perhaps that's the problem. I see Sybil's state of mind clearly. She is upset by the fact that a child died here in tragic circumstances. It's preying on her mind. When the dog gets out of control, or the central heating makes the house creak, or a bird flies into the window, she makes up her own fantasy about it. I think maybe she's right: she should see what she calls a head doctor."

The grin was almost vulpine: or was this now Cooling's imagination? Had he started to jump at shadows, translate the ciphers of the trade into substance, Gotterson into a Hollywood werewolf, changing with the moon into a monster?

As Cooling stood in the doorway, Gotterson touched his arm. "Do not think that I am unsympathetic," he said quietly. "Far from it. There is a strain for me also. One cannot just stand by and see one's own family suffer. I have even thought of moving house. An upheaval, but maybe that's what should be done. I have to keep a tight rein on myself, Mr. Cooling, otherwise I also would become distraught. I just do not understand what has been happening." His brow creased and there was a haunting flash of deep-seated worry in his eyes.

Gibbs, Harvester and Cheesman were at the monitors in his mother's living room. Watts had gone to the village, in his painter's overalls, to get some coffee.

"An admirable performance." He could not tell if Harvester was making fun of him.

"You should have chosen the theatre as an alternative career," said Gibbs.

In the kitchen he could hear his mother rattling about, her existence altered drastically by their presence, her world shrunken to the pair of bedrooms, the kitchen and a shared bathroom. Here in the living room the conditions had become almost siege-like, with the furniture pushed against the walls and their sleeping bags spread out in a neat row well clear of the monitors. Below, in the drive, stood one of the vans, disguised as the vehicle of a two-man decorating firm. At five each day one of the wiremen would drive it away, returning, unobserved, on foot, the process repeated each morning in reverse. As far as Mrs. Cooling's friends were concerned the flat was being redecorated.

He glanced at the monitors. Joseph was in his study, at the desk; Sybil played with Helen in front of the television set, leaving her from time to time, keeping an eye on kitchen matters. Brownie was with his master.

"When does it all start?" he asked, feeling immensely depressed at the inevitable.

"At about a quarter to six with any luck." Gibbs picked up a clipboard which lay on top of the central bank of monitor screens. "Harvester's been showing me what he'd like us to do."

Yes, Cooling thought, it would be Harvester, not himself nor Gibbs, who would be setting the pace and giving the orders. He listened patiently while Gibbs explained the first stage. They were hoping that Joseph would come through to watch the news on television, and if he did so alone—Sybil, they presumed, would be seeing to the child and the evening meal—they were to start "Feeding him the subliminals," as Harvester put it.

"Spool one," the psychiatrist told them. "Spool one of the video." If they cut into the normal programme with their own machine, the news would continue as usual, only every ten seconds, for the fleeting space of a tenth of a second, Joseph would be fed with a series of photographs: Hitler, Goebbels and Magda Goebbels in sequence. "You know and understand the theory?" asked Harvester, continuing as though he had not even posed the question. "The human eye will not be aware of the images, but the brain will assimilate them. Let's hope, gentlemen, that we have the subject alone and in front of that screen for a reasonable length of time to-night. It's essential that we should start him thinking about the past."

"If he's the trained and dedicated Nazi some would have us believe, those figures will be well entrenched anyway."

"Friend Cooling's a pessimist," Harvester chuckled. "The next series—which we'll use tonight if possible—is the whole of the Hitler investiture. Same speed: one frame every ten seconds and one tenth of a second. That should give him sweet dreams."

Unwittingly, Joseph Gotterson co-operated. While Sybil attended to the other matters, getting Helen to bed and preparing the meal, he sat for a full hour in front of the television set while Watts and Cheesman fed the video into the programme.

The couple ate dinner alone and talked, for most of the time, about the need to employ another girl in place of Marina. Cooling could not help but notice the patience and kindness which Joseph showed his wife, and the mutual trust they seemed to have one with the other.

Later that evening they both settled in the drawing room, Sybil curled up on the couch with a book, Joseph to watch a documentary.

"You think it's safe?" Gibbs asked—by this time all

pretence of Cooling being in charge had disappeared.

"With her in the room?" Harvester took off his wire-framed spectacles and set to polishing the lenses. "She's reading a book after all. Yes, run it, but if I tell you to cut out, do it at once. I'll only cut if she seems to become interested in the programme."

But Sybil remained deep in her book, so for the best part of an hour they fed Joseph subliminally with Adolf Hitler presenting the Iron Cross to the frightened Hitler Youth children in the garden of the Reich Chancellery. Harvester maintained that it was a good night's work.

For the next two days they were able to follow a similar pattern. Listening and watching during the daytime, following what appeared to be a very normal household with Joseph going on with his business long range, the telephone line between Pine Copse End and the offices of Scandinavian Imports buzzing constantly with news of sales, orders, bank statements, the handling of representatives and the arranging of meetings.

For two more nights they were able to catch Joseph alone in front of the television for nearly four hours, and in that time they continued to expose him to a wide selection of the tapes which Harvester had prepared.

On the second day, Cooling watched some of the material, run at normal speed, and deduced that the department had paid out a great deal of money for the operation. There were many individual photographs, including obvious shots of the bodies of the Goebbels family and people who had been around the bunker. But there were other, less obvious tapes which Harvester called "action replays." These had been set up with considerable care, using actors and backgrounds of stark reality which did not leave much to the imagination.

In one, the camera tracked through the grey concrete of the bunker, hesitated and then assumed a position near to a large metal door. It hovered there for a while before the door opened, revealing an all too lifelike Joseph and Magda Goebbels, both looking drawn and haggard, the woman in a state of near collapse. A man in SS uniform was with them and, as they passed through the door, the party paused, their mouths opening and closing in soundless conversation. One by one they reached forward, towards the camera, extending their arms as though to shake hands with someone unseen.

You did not have to be told that this was a reworking of that strange, almost unnecessary aside in Dr. Kunz's statement to the Russians. *As we left the study . . . two young persons in uniform, unknown to me, were sitting in the antechamber; one wore the uniform of the Hitler Youth . . . Goebbels and his wife said goodbye to the two . . .*

On another tape, the same pair of actors went through the gruesome actions of the suicide, though this was filmed more as an imagined sequence than reality. Again there was no sound (for that was impossible) but the background had about it a dreamlike quality, sharply angled shots, shadows projected in the occasional flashes of light as though from far away; other figures moved in when the two corpses lay still, and soon afterwards the flames rose up from the twin funeral pyres.

There was a sequence in which the camera appeared to drift through the seemingly endless passages of an underground shelter, occasionally passing groups of people, soldiers, officers, recognisable figures like Hitler, almost in shadow standing in a doorway with light behind him. From time to time faces came close to the camera, pausing, speaking words without sound.

Last of all a tall man, in greatcoat and officer's cap, made his way through a passage, the camera giving the impression of hurrying to keep up with the man, and set lower than him so that he appeared to be very tall. The officer climbed a concrete staircase, paused at the top to glance back, beckoning the camera on. Then out into a nightmare scene in which broken and sagging buildings seemed to overshadow everything, and the air was lit by continual flashes.

"How much of this will the brain retain if the eyes don't actually see it?" Cooling asked when the last tape had been run through.

"Practically everything." Harvester gave a pleased smirk. "And, of course, while the eyes are taking in the normal television programme they do see these frames.

They are simply unaware that they are seeing them. We did tests over the week-end with these films. The subjects we used could not understand why they had these vivid pictures in their minds. One of them had very bad dreams."

When they had finished on the third night, Harvester said that tomorrow would be the day for starting the sound.

It was during that night that Joseph Gotterson began to dream.

23

The first indication that something was wrong came at four minutes past three in the morning. Cooling dozed in front of the monitors while Cheesman did *The Times* crossword, leaning back in his chair, the headphones over his ears.

Cooling was pulled out of his half-sleep by a gentle shake on his knee.

"Headphones," murmured Cheesman, "I'm picking up a tapping noise. I think from the hall."

Cheesman had turned the audio-monitors onto the sneakies planted in the hall, and Cooling could hear it plainly, a gently knocking noise, the tapping irregular, both in pattern and volume.

"Movement," Cheesman said, drawing in his breath on the word.

Cooling's eyes went first to the screen which covered the stairs, taking a couple of seconds to realise that the movement was coming from the bedroom. Through the darkness he saw Sybil, a white shape, sitting up in bed, then gently swinging her body, her feet feeling for the floor, the rustling sounds magnified through the earphones. Cheesman had turned the volume up on the bedroom sneakies.

"She's coming on to the landing." Cooling felt himself short of breath. "Monitor the landing and hall audios."

They heard the noise of the door opening, the tapping still continuing in the hall, and on the screen Sybil moved silently forward to stand at the head of the stairs.

Only her back was visible to the lens, but she was undoubtedly listening, head cocked slightly, trying to gauge the source of the tapping, which, unless Cooling was getting a distortion, now appeared to be changing to a slight pattering—almost the noise of someone lightly bringing their hands together, still irregular, unrhythmic.

Without warning, Sybil turned so that her face was visible, straining, alert and undoubtedly anxious.

"She's hearing something else." Cooling could interpret the look. "She's hearing something upstairs. Bang all the audios up, see if we can sort it out."

Cheesman's hands moved over the tuners which poured all sounds reaching the distributed sneakies into their ears: a confused and overlapping mix—the pattering, the creaks of the fabric, Sybil's breathing and the rustle of her clothing, the steady breathing of Joseph in bed and Helen in her cot, the half-waking near whimper of Brownie down in the utility room.

"The bloody dog's going to start up in a minute."

Cheesman was fiddling with the tuners, trying to separate the various sounds, searching for the one which Sybil was obviously hearing close at hand. She had moved back now, almost to the bedroom door, fear taking the place of anxiety in her face.

"She's hearing the spook." Cheesman stated what was already obvious to Cooling.

"Get Harvester. Leave the audio and wake Harvester," Cooling whispered, craning forward, fascinated by the sight of Sybil Gotterson so clearly listening to sounds which were not audible on their equipment.

Cheesman slipped off the headphones and was halfway to the prone and sleeping figure of Harvester, picking his way in the dim light, when everything seemed to happen at once—Brownie began to howl, Helen started to whimper as she came out of sleep, and Joseph shouted loudly and clearly.

"No. No. The Russians are that way. We must go left here. Left."

Even with his knowledge of Werewolf it came as a shock to hear the German language coming, frantic, from Joseph's voice.

Sybil paused, unsure for a fraction of a second which way to move. It was certain that in this space of time the noises which she alone could hear were banished, and her indecision was split neatly between husband and child. The mother won, and Cooling saw her move away, almost running towards Helen's nursery. A moment later she was soothing the child, nursing her bad dream away and at the same time exorcising whatever demons she herself had feared.

Harvester was at Cooling's shoulder. "What did he shout? Cheesman said he was shouting in German."

Cooling told him, passing back a spare headset and pointing to the bedroom monitor. "He hardly stirred. I think he's still asleep."

As he said it, Joseph turned in the bed, restlessly, muttering.

"The left . . . My God . . . we're finished . . . children . . . the Führer . . . everybody." There was more, but it was all inaudible, wrapped around with groans and the sound of the bedclothes.

Downstairs, Brownie's howl subsided to a whimper.

"Thank heaven for that." Cheesman turned down the kitchen and utility audios.

"He called him the Führer," Harvester said quietly. "That's interesting. *The* Führer."

"Not Uncle," Cooling looked back at the psychiatrist.

"I wonder?" Harvester raked his fingers through tousled hair. "We've got to him, though, we've reached into his mind."

Cooling wondered what private hell was being relived inside Joseph's dreams, just as the sobbing began.

It came in small heaving sighs to start with, then a definite vocalising of deep grief. Helen was quiet now, and on the screens they saw Sybil, hesitating again on the landing.

The sobs from Joseph became interspersed with words, hardly intelligible. "Dead . . . all dead . . . my father and mother . . . Oh God in heaven to die like that . . . and the others . . . not like that . . . Oh my God . . ." and on into a ramble in which the words took second place to the noises of grief.

Sybil switched on the main bedroom light, and they caught sight of her face shadowed with anxiety as she went towards the bed and her husband, throwing herself across the covers, slipping an arm around his shoulders.

"Joseph, you're dreaming, darling. Wake up. Come on."

He surfaced from sleep with a long shudder, and even with the lack of definition from the pin lens they could see that his face was stained with tears.

"What?" he cried loudly. "What? Where're the . . . ? Angel?"

"It's all right. You were dreaming. It's all right, darling."

He let out a long groan of mingled relief and sorrow, neither emotion truly distinguishable from the other.

"Angel, I'm sorry. Terrible. A terrible nightmare."

"I know. It's nightmare time for everybody. Helen wakened, and Brownie."

"Did I wake them? I'm sorry."

"No, it all came at once. I was having one of my dreams as well."

"I'm sorry." He kept repeating it as though the words were taped inside his head on an endless loop.

"You're sweating, you're drenched in sweat." Sybil practical, wiping his streaming face with a tissue. "I've never known you to have dreams like this before. Was it horrible?"

"I used to have dreams as a child—nightmares, I mean. Not for years, though, not for a very long time."

"You want to talk about it?"

There was a long pause as he leaned on one elbow looking at her. "I've been very lucky, Angel, finding you when I did. Was your dream terrible also?"

"Just the noises," she gave a small nervous laugh. "The things you think are foolish. Tapping noises, pattering, then the crying voice a long way off. It could have been half-way around the world, it sounded so far off."

He leaned forward and kissed her with extreme gentleness. Cooling took his eyes from the screen. "My dream came from half-way around the world also; and from another time."

"Tomorrow," Harvester whispered in Cooling's ear, "we'll start using the audios."

24

It was plain to all of them that Joseph Gotterson was showing signs of a man who was both distressed and on the edge of confusion. As they watched him throughout the next day the marks of a split in his character were clear.

"You notice how the punch and drive are going out of him in matters of business?" Harvester commented. "You see before you a man who is dredging up unpleasant memories from the past."

It was certainly incredible to see how the few carefully implanted subliminal ideas had altered Joseph's attack and attitude. In the night, when Sybil had wakened him from his dream, he had already shown the first signs of a new reliance upon her. During the day which followed, he faced long periods of indecision, as though only part of his mind was operating on the conscious level.

On three occasions he gave instructions to Miss Anerson at the office of Scandinavian Imports, only to ring back shortly afterwards to alter his orders. He paced up and down in the large studio, aimless and brooding. He seemed to hesitate over even small matters, like moving from one room to another. Helen irritated him, something they had never seen before, and, during lunch, he hardly spoke to either the child or his wife, though he did reach out to Sybil, twice, gripping her shoulder with his hand, as if to reassure himself of her reality.

Early in the day, Harvester had made certain that the first audio was set on the machine in readiness—a short tape marked simply with a red figure one on the cassette. Towards late afternoon he gave more detailed instructions.

"We'll let him have it just as he's leaving his study. I want it piped through his right hand speaker, the one nearest the door; then we'll do it again, with the volume up slightly when he gets through to the drawing room—through our speaker in his television. You'll have to boost the volume a little," he cautioned Watts, who was on duty at the monitors. "It's not a loud piece but I want him to hear it above the television sound."

They also had a tape on the video link—the one that meandered through the bunker—which Harvester wanted to play subliminally while Joseph watched the news.

Just before a quarter to six, Joseph Gotterson began to tidy his desk. It was time to finish for the day, he told himself. Maybe he should have finished earlier. He wondered if this depression had something to do with the dream last night. Sybil had told him that he had called out, shouted, in his sleep and he had a nagging worry that maybe he had done so in German. He could not deny that this was a fear which had haunted him for a long time—talking in his sleep. Common sense told him that he would probably revert to his natural language under unconscious stress. He would prefer to keep that fact from Sybil: it was not necessary—at least not yet necessary—for her to know about the past.

It was the past which had suddenly sprung back to haunt him in the last few days: all the things which he had thought were long buried seemed to be springing up too readily into his head: a bubbling spring of dreamlike memories, most of which seemed unreal. All the old questions and uncertainties now swamped the hopes and plans for a great future.

He switched off his desk light, glanced around and began to walk slowly towards the door, his mind full of the vivid memories. Should he perhaps see a doctor? But what could he tell him? What story could he concoct to present the correct symptoms to a doctor? His hand reached out for the doorknob.

Across the road in the flat at Heath Corner, Harvester tapped Watts' shoulder and the wireman's finger pressed down on the transmit key.

Joseph went rigid with fear, glancing back into the room, almost expecting to see a figure standing there. Not knowing if he imagined it or whether it was just another of these vivid memories? Was it even a memory—this strange voice in his head which had come like a whisper?

"Helmut, die Kinder werden eine Fahrt machen. Eine traum nach Schwanenwerder." A woman speaking quite fast, but very far away, faint. "Helmut, the children will be going on a journey. A dream journey to Schwanenwerder."

He leaned against the door, hardly daring to move, his heart pounding, knowing that he had heard a voice quite clearly and fearing the madness which might be coming with it.

In the flat at Heath Corner, Cooling felt his hair literally rise on the back of his neck: a cold shiver passing from head to foot. Like the others listening on their headsets, he had heard the woman's whisper—the promised dream journey to Schwanenwerder, the Goebbelses' most loved island home where little Helmut had spent many happy hours. The dream journey which, according to some reports, Magda Goebbels had told the children about. They had not believed her and had to be dragged screaming to receive the fatal injections.

Cooling now saw Joseph's reaction to the whisper,

the sudden pull up, stopped in his tracks as though the almost inaudible voice had gone into his head with the force of a bullet. For a second he turned, swinging, one-handed, from the brass doorknob, his face blank puzzlement, a man on the brink of chaos, not knowing if the voice was a projection of his deepest thoughts, something half-recalled from the hidden past, or, and this must now have been his worst fear, some dreadful reality spun from the grave and present here and now in this house: this room.

Harvester had not prepared them for the texture of the recording, the chilling timbre of the woman's voice, a fading hollow echo which could easily be mistaken for a thought passing through the head, particularly in the mind of a distracted man.

Joseph dragged his study door open, and for a few seconds was out of their sight on the monitors as he passed along the short passage connecting the study to the drawing room.

Helen was already being bathed upstairs and the television remained on, the BBC news about to start. But when Joseph Gotterson finally emerged into the drawing room, he appeared to have no real interest in the television, slumping into a chair and gazing at the screen with watery eyes which almost certainly did not take in the transmitted images.

Harvester gave an abrupt order to Watts. "Video," and the subliminal film was locked into the television. Again at one tenth of a second, every ten seconds, the frames overlapped the newscaster and their latest reports. He signalled once more, and, for the second time, the wireman's finger pressed down on the audio key.

The woman's voice hissed quickly through the headphones, projected a shade above the volume of the television, into the drawing room and Joseph's unbelieving ears.

"*Helmut, Heide, wo seid ihr? Wo seid ihr Hilde, Helga?*" Magda Goebbels calling for her children from the grave.

This time Joseph became acutely confused. Instead of bewilderment, though, plain terror showed fleetingly across his face. Half rising from the chair, he peered about him, part of his mind convinced of what he had heard, yet another part uncertain, trying to force some logic into the situation.

"Close down," Harvester murmured, and Gibbs leaned forward to tap the wireman's shoulder. "I don't want to push him too hard." He set about polishing the lenses of his spectacles again. It occurred to Cooling that this was almost an obsession with him, a habit as some men will stroke their eyebrows or pull their ears. "We're taking him very close," Harvester continued. "Tomorrow, maybe, we can give him the whole works." He turned to Cooling, "What's the chance of getting the wife and child out of the house tomorrow afternoon?"

"I don't know. You've been monitoring them. Have they suggested anything?"

Watts shook his head.

"Perhaps," said Gibbs, "your mother might beg a lift from her into Farnham."

"Well, you can suggest it." Cooling felt rage burning in his cheeks. "On the other hand, why don't you waltz over there and ask them out for a tea party? Please, Mrs. Gotterson, come out to tea with your daughter so that my spooks can destroy your husband."

"We're doing this operation as a result of a Ministerial request." Harvester did not even look at Cooling, his hands sorting through the metal box of tapes and cassettes. "It would be right to remember that. I'm only trying to be humane, Cooling. It could get unpleasant if the woman and child were in the house."

"What are you actually going to do?"

"Freak the dog." He might have been making a casual statement regarding some everyday chore. "Freak the dog and then pour audios into the house."

"And use the transducers," added Gibbs. "Wait till he starts shouting and play his shouts back to him."

"Instant haunt."

"My God, I hope it's worth it."

"It'll be worth it." Harvester turned to Gibbs. "See if the old lady can winkle them out. If it's going to be possible, I would suggest that the Deputy Director comes down." Then, as an afterthought, "He'd better bring a couple of confessors with him. Friend Gotter-

son might feel like telling his story and I'd prefer he
talked to qualified people. I've got enough medical
equipment here and my technician's a trained nurse."

"Nurse and lion tamer, no doubt." It seemed to Cooling that the technician had been kept well in the background since Harvester's arrival.

"Yes," Harvester was unruffled, "he's done a spot of
lion taming in his time."

Gibbs disappeared into the other part of the flat
while Cooling stood by and watched the monitors. Joseph had come out of his first bewilderment, the hyper-
tension diminishing, leaving him in a jumpy, unsettled
state.

"Confusion still apparent," Harvester said. "Leave
him alone and he'll come to us like a lamb."

Gibbs returned. "She's calling them now."

As he spoke the telephone in Pine Copse End started
to ring. Sybil was coming down the stairs, almost col-
liding with Joseph as he leaped from the drawing
room.

Cooling tried to ignore the fact that it was his
mother's voice at the other end of the line, magnified
through the speakers.

"Sybil dear, this is a terrible cheek, but I rang to ask
if by any chance you were going into Farnham tomorrow afternoon." All so bloody normal. Cooling remembered Maitland-Wood's comment that his mother
would have worked well in the trade.

"Well, I can. I have to go down sometime tomorrow. What is it you wanted?"

"The wretched bus service is so irregular and I've got a dental appointment at three. I just thought there would be no harm in asking you."

"Well, of course I'll take you down. I'll go and do the bit of shopping I've got to get. What time would you want to come back?"

"I won't be many minutes—to tell you the truth . . ." and she went on into a long and most personal description of the problems she had been having with her dental plate. "Could I give you and Helen tea afterwards?"

"Back at your flat? That would be lovely."

"No, I thought it might be nice if I took you out to tea. Helen would like that, wouldn't she? I know a place where they do splendid cakes."

It was all settled in a matter of five minutes, including a certain amount of garrulous chatter.

"Better alert Maitland-Wood." Harvester nodded to Gibbs.

Cooling stifled a sigh and went through to the bathroom. Though he had done little during the day, he now suddenly felt tired. It was a fatigue which seemed to come from the very fact of living with the business: living and watching. He realised with some dismay that he had not rung Steph for two days. She would be wondering about him and might even try to get him on his mother's phone.

When he went through with his coat his mother was

in the hall. "It's all getting quite exciting dear, isn't it? Nothing's going to happen to Sybil or the child, though, Mr. Gibbs tells me."

"No." He wondered what Gibbs meant by nothing happening to them. Whatever the outcome of tomorrow's assault on Joseph's memory, nothing could ever be the same for them again, and it depressed him to think of them, in ignorance and innocence, making small plans for part of their lives which might have no true future. "I don't think we'll be here much longer, Mum. It must be a trial for you. Sorry you've been involved."

"Not at all, dear. Not at all. It's been quite thrilling really. Like the telly."

Yes, he thought, just like the telly: a small charade to brighten up her life. He smiled and kissed her, pulling on his coat and passing out of the flat, down into the drive and up towards the village with the waiting telephone box.

As he walked past the dark outline of Pine Copse End, with its lights bright in the windows, he realised, with something of a shock, that he had unwillingly become deeply involved in the daily lives of the Gottersons. It was as if the operation had removed one of the walls of the house and allowed them to be seen, as a zoologist sees animals in their natural state. In a few days of unobserved watching, he had come to know the small habits of their living together; the things which appeared to make them into a family: the patience

they both shared, their obvious concern and regard for
each other and for the child; Sybil's acceptance of her
role, as wife and mother, which would be thought of as
subservient by many women of her age; Joseph's almost dedicated dynamism, which seemed to be chan-
nelled into the somewhat pedestrian business of selling
Scandinavian furniture to a country which was doing
its best to resist imports; how they spoke to one another; how they ate; their likes and dislikes; their sharing; their endearments; the varied centres of the little
world they were so obviously trying to build at Pine
Copse End.

It struck him most forcibly, as he turned from
Scholars Road into Cricket Lane, that the whole aura
surrounding them was one of complete normality. Had
Harvester or Gibbs not seen this? Or had they seen it
and ignored it because the Minister wanted Joseph
Gotterson out, and Maitland-Wood desperately needed
to know what role the man had really played during
those final hours in the Führer-bunker thirty years before.

As he neared the telephone box he thought about
Steph and what he had learned from the Gottersons.
Could he and Steph build a world for themselves and
live together with that same sense of patience and
affection? Would she be able to throw off the demands
of a career for the new demands: or could she combine
the two?

When he finally heard her voice on the line, Cooling

realised that he had not rung too soon. She had that relieved edge in her words and questions.

"I was starting to get a little worried. I thought you might have run off abroad without telling me."

"Should be through in a couple of days now." As he said it, Cooling cursed silently.

"Through? Through what?" She picked it up, worrying at it. He would never be able to deceive Steph.

"I mean that she's much better. Going out tomorrow. I should be able to get back to London in a couple of days."

"I've got four free days as from tomorrow." She left the fact hanging between them, the inference obvious. "Would you like me to come down and pick you up?"

Cooling's mind was full of wasted time and the desire to achieve normality. During his career as an evaluator he had hardly questioned the over-all aim, the total idea of democracy enshrined in the system of government. Now he wondered. When it was all boiled down, his aim in life was some kind of safety, privacy, the old chestnut of middle-class freedom to choose within a fair and honest society. Now he wanted to make that choice with Steph.

"If I finish tomorrow, I'll give you a call. It would be nice to drive back with you."

"And we will be able to make plans, then?"

"I think so. I expect so."

"You haven't heard about your posting, then?"

"No. No, not yet."

"Have you asked anyone?" There seemed to be a hint of criticism, as though she was on the point of accusing him for things not done.

"I've told them that I want to organise my future. That I'm thinking about getting married."

"I bet they loved that. With my track record."

"They're not worried by it."

He wondered how they might take his resignation, and if he did opt out what he could expect of his life. Even when novelists wrote about the department, they told the truth these days. It was like the Communist Party or the Church of Rome, they did not just let you leave. They clung to your soul, wrestled over it and with it for your own salvation. So what was democracy? The right to choose? Yet the opposing extreme factions gave you as little choice now as the large conflicting ideologies. The far left wanted you controlled by the state, the far right by the idea of choice.

"I love you, Vincent," she said, without emotion or passion: a simple expression of what was true.

"And I you," a statement and a choice. It was the first real choice he had made for years. As for the Gottersons they could make no choice: no decisions or selections. Maitland-Wood and his obsession saw to that, and the history together with the system backed up with its watertight cut-outs, its barricades of typewriters and memos, forms and instructions. Once they had you in the system there was little escape, only degrees, a shift of emphasis at each general election. The power remained constant. "About my posting," he hesitated. "I might just try to post myself out of it altogether."

As he walked back down Cricket Lane, he knew that he had said the wrong thing, that Steph would start to worry at it, perhaps even precipitate matters.

25

Maitland-Wood arrived just before two-thirty. As he put it, "in good time for the show." Cooling's mother was due to go over to Pine Copse End at quarter-to-three, and she had promised that Sybil and the child would not get back until around six.

"Three hours'll do you, will it?" the Deputy Director asked, and Harvester nodded. "Ample time for the main event."

There was another man with Maitland-Wood, stooping and bald, in his mid-fifties, dressed like a provincial bank manager of the old school: navy blue suit with a little shine. Harvester knew him at once.

"You haven't got Crown with you?" he asked.

"You're here," Maitland-Wood told him as though it explained everything. "This has already cost a lot of money. It's time for doubling up. You've got a technician. Surely you can work together."

Harvester grunted, and the new arrival gave a smug smile. "We've done it before."

Harvester agreed. Confessors usually worked in pairs so they had a full set.

By half-past two the living room had filled up; the wiremen seated at the monitors; Cooling, Gibbs and Harvester standing behind them, the atmosphere like that of some theatrical control room just before the curtain was due to rise. They did not talk much, except for Maitland-Wood, who made remarks about the sensitivity of the equipment and his hope that they would get it over and done with that afternoon.

"I've asked the Minister to stand by," he told them, redolent with self-importance; the man who had a direct link with the oracle.

Cooling merely felt numb, his mind a blank but for the repetitious thought that it was all a waste of time, money, effort and, maybe, people.

Joseph worked in his study, restless, nervous, jumping at the least sound, prone to staring vacantly, seeing ghosts visible only to his mind.

Sybil changed in the bedroom, and Cooling was conscious, not for the first time, of turning his head away from the screens as she stripped to her underwear. He did not even question this odd puritanism but felt uncomfortable at the muttered comments of Cheesman and Watts. They were more appreciative than bawdy, but Cooling found it strangely embarrassing. He thought of the couple in the grass all those years ago, and the few women with whom he had shared intimacy.

Just before a quarter-to-three the doorbell rang in Pine Copse End and Helen, who had been quietly playing with a favourite toy, hurled herself towards the front door and struggled with the knob shouting to her mother that it was Mrs. Cooling, which in her baby voice came out as Mrs. Cooing.

Cooling's mother stayed with the child, helping her into her little coat while Sybil went through to the study.

"You won't be too long," Joseph seemed to be almost pleading.

"We're just going to do some shopping and have tea out. You said you'd be all right."

"Yes. Yes, I'll be fine, Angel." Uncertain, all the old confidence sapped, the nerves bare.

"You've got Brownie. He's good company."

The dog stirred from his place beside Joseph's desk, hearing his name and thinking for a moment that he was to be given a run. Joseph reached down and patted him, running his hand along the animal's flanks and muttering quietening words.

"You will be okay," Sybil repeated. Then, as she kissed him on the cheek, "It's those dreams, isn't it? Don't you think you ought to see a doctor?"

"Maybe, Angel. Yes, maybe I should see a doctor. I thought it was all over—the past—but it seems to have come back. Perhaps you're right. Perhaps it's this house."

She closed in on him again, affectionately, resting a cheek against his. "We won't be long." As she turned away the camera caught her face and Cooling saw that her brow was creased with worry.

"Do we have to?" Cooling turned towards Maitland-Wood.

"What d'you mean, Vincent? Going soft, are you? We have to know."

"Well, let me go over and ask him straight. Do we need to go through this creepy business?"

Harvester spoke. "Do you imagine for a moment that he's going to cough it all out without some pressure? Now it's started we have to finish it."

It was absurd, thought Cooling. Absurd and in some ways obscene, this oblique hammering into the man's mind. The tools of the trade seemed to have become almost part of a way of life. He saw Sybil leaving the study, reappearing on the drawing-room monitor, and it occurred to him that it was the way of life now in the mid-seventies. Every family eavesdropped each night when they watched events around the world on their cosy screens. Privacy was dead and the past could never be buried, for it was now carefully being built up, in either fact or fiction, ready for instant replays while the spectators sat and ate frozen dinners or chewed on chemical chocolate bars. A world of voyeurs.

The front door closed, and the hidden cameras looked out on the silent empty hall and stairs, the bedroom, drawing room, kitchen and the inhabited study where Joseph, distracted from his normal routine, sat at his desk, the Alsatian dozing by his side.

"We'll give him five minutes." Harvester's voice was throaty, like a man, Cooling thought, on the verge of sexual excess.

There was a timelessness about the short wait, as if Joseph was stuck, preserved in some invisible jelly, and the other rooms lay silent, ready for the final drama, the whole house growing dark as the winter daylight faded into the early twilight of mid-afternoon.

Harvester twitched at Cooling's elbow, turning to look around before asking if everyone was ready. Cheesman and Watts nodded, while Maitland-Wood grunted to him to get on. Gibbs remained silent.

"Right," Harvester quiet and clear now as though the phlegm had been cleared from his throat. "Right, let's start with the dog."

On the panel in front of the central monitor screen there was a small switch above a tuner, the whole marked with a Dymo label—*High-Frequency*. Cheesman reached forward, moved the switch and started to increase the volume with the tuner. A needle climbed on one of the dials, then steadied. They would hear nothing strange, no audible sound in headphones or from the sneakies, for the hidden high-frequency amplifiers would now be emitting a call which was too high for human ears, a noise which would only reach the dog's hearing in an explosion of unbearable sound.

The animal reacted instantly, and Cooling wondered how much pain they were inflicting, as Brownie raised himself, as though pulled upwards by hidden wires, his front legs off the ground and mouth open in a strange horrible cry, an almost human scream.

Joseph, who had been sitting still in the same wax-work position, leaped out of his chair, moving downwards towards the dog as Cheesman cut the switch.

The dog still turned its head from side to side, as though the high-frequency tone remained inside his brain, the awful cry now reduced to a frightened whimper as his master tried to soothe him and, in Heath Corner, Watts pressed the audio key.

It was a man's voice, a whisper like that of the woman, there one minute and then gone, in German. "The Führer is to honour you with a medal."

Joseph remained still as death, caught in the act of bending over the dog, his head raised, eyes wide, un-believing.

Then Cheesman pressed the high-frequency key again and the dog went wild, threshing to and fro, rolling over as if trying to stop the sound audible only to him. Joseph shouted, "Brownie, Brownie," the horror on his face now split between concern for the animal and his own incredulity.

Watts pressed the audio key again and it was the woman's voice—"Do not bother Uncle Adolf."

Brownie was howling, running berserk around the study, ready to crash through the wall if it was possible to rid his ears of the sound, the howl rising and now joined by Joseph's screams.

Then the man's voice, louder, though still a whisper, "The future is in your hands. You are our investment in the future."

Joseph's scream became one long negative—"No," starting high and descending the scale, his own hands over his ears as he ran towards the study door and, at the same moment, the crazed dog leaped for him, fangs bared and frothing, the head rolling and eyes wide, the noise from his throat a combination of pain and anger.

Cooling heard himself shout and was conscious of Harvester impatiently telling him to be quiet; Cheesman's hand crossing over and cutting the high-frequency signal though it seemed to make little difference to the dog now. Joseph was scrabbling on the floor, one arm clawing up towards the knob while Brownie bit away at his other shoulder, fastening his jaws around the screaming man.

Harvester muttered something and then said, "The transducers."

Watts' hands moved to the switches which activated these instruments so that everything picked up by the sneakies was fed back and amplified at high volume into the house, so that the shouts and the dog's howling became huge echoes of their reality.

"Tape four," Harvester's voice like an icicle as the audio key was once more depressed and both amplifiers in the study, together with the one in the television set, became the source of yet another, and entirely new, sequence of sounds—the roar of guns and shells, sometimes close, sometimes dull nearby thuds, but all picked up and fed back with the other noises, through the hidden transducers.

Joseph's hand, grabbed tightly on the doorknob, pushing and throwing open the way to escape. Brownie, distracted by the action, let go his hold for a moment, paused, growling, and leaped forward sliding and slithering on the polished parquet of the passage through to the drawing room. As he did so, the telephone in the flat at Heath Corner rang.

In the midst of the hellish noise beating through the earphones and the one, tuned-down amplifier, Cooling expected the call to be for him. He knew it must be Steph, yet he could not allow his eyes to leave the monitors—the dog baying and scratching at the drawing-room door and Joseph staggering breathless, hands to his head through the study passageway, emerging in the drawing room.

He was conscious of the Deputy Director answering the telephone and then shouting to Harvester, "Kill it all. No. His wife's on her way back. The car's broken down." Then, as Cooling turned, "Your mother. Calling from the village."

He saw the hands moving, like the hands of musicians, across the switches and tuners, heard the sounds dying, except for the constant howl of the dog, and Joseph's groans.

Harvester swore, mingling with Joseph, who had now begun to shout at the dog as he crabbed his way across the drawing room towards the door.

Brownie cringed for a moment and then started a belligerent growl, settling back, preparing to spring again. But Joseph reached the door first, throwing it open, and in that moment Cooling was distracted by the hallway monitor screen, a shadow across the glass in the porchway and the sound of a key in the lock.

"Jesus Christ," Cooling shouted, and turned towards the door of his mother's living room as the corner of his eye caught the terrible sight of the front door at Pine Copse End opening, of Sybil revealed in the porch and of little Helen running in to greet the wild and uncontrolled Brownie.

. As he tore the door open he even heard her voice, laughing, "Come on, Brownie, good boy . . ." and then the sharp bark and the scream, Joseph shouting and Sybil yelling in the background.

26

He knew that the technician—the lion tamer—was at his heels as he crashed down the stairs and out into the dull and rapidly darkening afternoon. As he reached the drive of Pine Copse End he could hear the screams which made him push harder, running as he had not run for years. Then, suddenly, he was there, in the porch with Joseph and Sybil vainly trying to pull the dog from the pathetic little bundle in the hall.

Cooling pushed through and grabbed at the animal's collar. As he did so, another hand joined his—the technician behind him—and they both heaved as though to an order. The dog gave a long yelping whimper which dissolved into a growl and bark of anger, but he let go of the child.

As the technician's foot came up hard the dog turned

in the narrow porch, ready to spring again to the attack.

The noise behind them was confused, Joseph hysterical, Sybil's voice cloaked with sobs, and Cooling realised that over in the other house some fool had not switched off the transducers.

He was hardly aware of the technician's hand coming up, or of the revolver, just the shock of the explosion and the final loud whimper from the dog as it was lifted into the air and smashed against the porch to drop twitching on the tiles.

Joseph was babbling in German and Sybil bent over the child. There was blood, Cooling could see, and Helen lay terribly still.

"For Christ's sake, get an ambulance and a doctor," he shouted at the technician. But there was no need, Harvester and Gibbs were in the porch, Harvester pushed them out of the way to kneel by the still child.

Sybil stood speechless, her eyes wide as she looked on, helpless. Then Harvester rose and said something to the technician, who left without question.

"We'll take your car." Harvester looked at Gibbs, then at Sybil. "She'll be all right. Shock, bruising and some bites to the shoulder. He didn't get her throat. Mr. Gibbs'll take you to the hospital. We'll telephone on ahead."

The child started to whimper and Sybil dropped to her knees, "Can I move her?"

"Gently." Harvester switched to Cooling. "Get that bloody dog covered up. Don't let the child see that."

Cooling stripped off his jacket and heard Sybil saying "It's all right, darling. Helen, it's all right." Then, as realising it for the first time, "Joseph? What's the matter with my husband? What in heaven's name . . . ?"

"We'll take care of him, Mrs. Gotterson. He's in shock. He's had a bad experience."

Cooling bent to cover the dog's corpse as Joseph made his first coherent remark. "Blondi," he said. "Blondi. They poisoned Blondi. They didn't shoot him. It's wrong." Then in German, "My God, what's to become of us now? With the Führer gone."

"You'll be all right," said Harvester, putting an arm around his shoulders. "We'll look after you now. We'll give you something to eat."

"Where's my medal?" asked Joseph.

"Safe enough."

The technician had returned and moved to the other side. Together they led Werewolf back into his drawing room. They had switched off the transducers now, and Cooling noticed that Gibbs did not meet his eye as he came in through the porch to help carry the, now sobbing, child out to his car.

As Gibbs drove away, the confessor, who had arrived with Maitland-Wood, came up the drive.

"They're inside," Cooling said, looking at him with distaste, then turned and followed him into the house. When the drawing-room door closed, Cooling went over to the telephone and stood looking directly up at where the pin lens scanned the hall.

"I'm resigning," he said loudly. "As from this moment I'm out." Then he dialled Steph's number.

The Deputy Director had other ideas. "You may well have called your young woman down here," he said, standing in the hall ten minutes later, "but you are not yet free of your obligations to us." He jabbed Cooling in the chest gently. "I don't think we'd want you any more, not on a permanent basis, but while I'm here you'll finish this up and you'll go when I say you can go and not before." His hand rested on the drawing-room door. "Don't you want to hear the truth, Vincent?"

"What truth?"

"Werewolf."

"What's the truth about him any more? Do you really think it'll make any difference to anything? You did what you wanted. You tilted him, tore off his balls, almost killed his child."

"I thought you'd be interested."

He pushed open the door, and as he did so Harvester appeared from the other side motioning him back into the hall.

"Well?" asked Maitland-Wood, anxious, like a man awaiting news of an operation or a medical test.

Harvester shook his head. "Not yet." He took off the glasses and began polishing them again, the constant gesture.

"How long, for God's sake?"

"Oh, he was there," Harvester patient, even gentle. "But it was a long time ago. He was the Hitler Youth boy, I've little doubt about that. But I don't think his memory is absolutely clear. My guess is that they primed him after the breakout. When he was in shock. Told him that he was Helmut Goebbels. But it's all deeply buried. He's not really certain who he is."

"But he is the inheritor? The hope for the future of the party?"

For a moment he sounded as though he needed to believe it; needed Werewolf to be the Nazi phoenix, as if his own future was somehow linked with the ideal.

"I doubt it." Harvester's manner was gentle. "Oh, I think some crackbrained fanatics saw him as that, but as for him . . . ? No. For Joseph Gotterson the past is dead. Or was dead. Blotted out until you raised it again. Just now he was quite lucid. He told me that all he ever wanted was to forget his childhood and the first years of his life after Berlin." He shrugged. "We'll find out the truth, but at this stage I believe that all he wanted was peace and his wife and child. A chance to let the past bury itself and not intrude into the future. I get the impression that he was vastly ashamed of his childhood."

"But . . . ?" Maitland-Wood's mouth sagged.

"He was a little boy when it all happened. We've dug up a particularly nasty horror which has been dormant for a long time."

"How bad is he?" asked Cooling, sick and disgusted so that it showed in his manner and speech.

"Confused. Lucid for only short periods. The rest of the time he's back in the bunker."

Cooling thought of the self-possessed Joseph Gotterson and then the shadow of the man he had seen grovelling, cowering near his injured child.

"He called the dog Blondi. Hitler's dog."

Harvester nodded. "He's going through a nightmare. God knows how much of it he saw back in '45. Certainly he saw the bodies."

The drawing-room door opened and the other confessor came out.

"He's quieter. Wants his medal. I've let him go through to the study. He says it's there."

"Merciful Jesus," said Cooling.

"There's a bloody pistol there—in the drawer." Maitland-Wood was into the drawing room moving quite fast, compact in the moment of action.

"My fellow's with him," called Harvester, almost indifferent to Maitland-Wood's anxiety.

Then the two shots exploded from the study, a pause between them allowing the Deputy Director to reach the passage just as the second crashed out.

Cooling heard Maitland-Wood give a low grunt as he passed through the door and was conscious of Harvester starting to move across the room.

The technician was still breathing when they got to him, but there was no chance for Gotterson. He lay on his back at the far side of the desk, the top of his head a sponge of blood, the pistol still in his hand.

Cooling did not have to join Maitland-Wood beside the body to know the fact of death. There was a vivid montage of thoughts and pictures in his head—the photographs of the dead and charred bodies of Goebbels and his wife in the garden of the Reich Chancellery, the pathetic row of dead children in their nightclothes, and the omnipresent picture of Moonlight and the child Werewolf climbing across the rubble on their way to freedom. It all ended here in this red-brick house in quiet Surrey.

Later, the technician, who had caught the bullet in the upper part of his chest, told them that Gotterson had behaved calmly and with no sign of his first hysteria. He had talked only of the medal and the technician had let him go, alone, to the desk. The gun had come as a surprise.

"I don't think he would have done anything about me but I went forward to tackle him," he said.

"Did he tell you anything? Did he say anything?" pressed Maitland-Wood, still desperate for some sign of the things he wished to believe.

They had the man propped up in Harvester's arms, waiting for the ambulance.

"Something about his father." The technician was weak and in shock, his face grey with pain. "I don't know. I think he shouted that he was going to join his father."

What ghosts, Cooling reflected, would be made of this? What ghosts and shadows would be stirred in Maitland-Wood's mind and the minds of Sybil Gotterson and her child?

Did Helmut die in the bunker all those years ago? Or, like his father before him, die by his own hand here and now? Or was the blasted corpse that of a young lad who showed great courage in 1945 fighting to defend his city? Did it matter now? The words of Pontius Pilate came into his head again—What is truth? It depended, he supposed, on where you were standing at a certain time and on a certain date in history.

27

It was not quite the end. An ambulance came and took away the technician, who would live. Later a plain van removed Joseph Gotterson's body. Maitland-Wood spoke with Cooling's mother, who agreed to break the news to Sybil. Gibbs fussed a little and the others stood around looking nervous, worried and grave.

For a while the police were in evidence and there were telephone calls to London. The local press were already on to the fact that a tragedy had occurred, and the right stories had to be sorted. The house would have to be stripped, the Deputy Director said. Everything had to come out as soon as possible, though nobody offered to start work straight away.

Steph arrived, bewildered at the activity, pressing Cooling for the truth, though eventually she reluctantly

accepted that there had been a serious accident connected with the trade.

At around eight o'clock Cooling managed to get a
few words with his mother, who, by this time, looked
white, frail and in shock.

"They said nothing would happen to Sybil and the
child," she kept repeating.

"It's the innocent who always get mangled." Cooling
knew it was a platitude but his mother nodded her
head gravely. She was a woman whose generation had
been brought up on platitudes, and she had really
believed that there would be blue birds over the white
cliffs of Dover in 1945.

"I only thought they wanted to question him. You
said it was nothing serious," looking at him as though
he had been both cause and effect. "When the car
broke down and we had to walk back to the village, I
instinctively felt I should telephone. I told Sybil that
I'd call the dentist from the phone box. She wanted me
to come back to the house."

"You did the right thing, Mother. You probably
saved the child's life."

All he wanted was to get away, out of it, back to
London with Steph.

But Maitland-Wood and Gibbs were firm. The police
required statements from everyone. It had to be official
and Cooling would make his contribution in the morning. They made it quite clear that the statement would

adhere to department policy. When Cooling mentioned whitewash they shrugged.

Makeshift arrangements were made for passing the night and nobody, except the Deputy Director, was allowed back to town. The others—apart from Harvester, who had friends in the area—would shake down at Heath Corner.

In the middle of this frustration, Cooling asked about Sybil. She was being kept in the hospital with the child. They would see about compensation in due course. Nobody objected to the idea of Cooling sleeping at Pine Copse End. Gibbs even seemed quite pleased that there would be someone occupying the house, and Steph raised no problems. After all, she did not know the history.

He made sure that all the monitors were disconnected: too many lives had already been peeped into and too many heads opened for examination. At around nine he took Steph off to the local pub, where they sat alone at a table, drank wine and worked their way through a plate of ham sandwiches. When they had done, Cooling took her back to the Gottersons' bedroom, where they lay for a long time, wrapped around each other talking of the future. Sleep came quite easily in the end.

The luminous hands on his watch showed that it was a little before three-thirty when he woke to the tapping. It was the same noise that Sybil Gotterson had heard: the noise that he had listened to on the headphones. Yet, here, in the bedroom, it sounded clear, distinct and urgent.

Steph remained asleep, curled into an embryonic ball at his side, and it was not until he was half-way to the bedroom door that Cooling realised he was following the same pattern as that of Sybil Gotterson on the night of Joseph's dream.

This time there was no light on the landing, but when he switched it on, the regular tapping appeared to get louder and more persistent. He knew what it was, now: the noise made by a child bouncing a rubber ball on the ground or against a wall.

Then he became aware of the singing, faint snatches as though drifting from a long way off. As Sybil had said, they were faint enough to be coming from half-way around the world.

In a cold sweep of horror, he began to decipher the words from the fragments. A nursery rhyme sung far away, yet there in the house. Sung in triumph as though a great childish victory had been won. Then not one song but several, laced together so that only different lines and words were audible from the distant, present piping voice:

> All the king's horses and all the king's men,
> Couldn't put Humpty together again . . .
> The maid was in the garden . . .
> . . . down came a blackbird . . .
> Pecked . . . Pecked . . . Pecked . . .
> Hark, hark, the dogs do bark . . .